BOX TOP
Dreams

Miriam Glassman

A Yearling Book

Published by
Bantam Doubleday Dell Books for Young Readers
a division of
Random House, Inc.
1540 Broadway
New York, New York 10036

Visit us on the Web! www.randomhouse.com

**Educators and librarians, for a variety of teaching tools, visit us
at www.randomhouse.com/teachers**

ISBN: 0-440-41417-2

Reprinted by arrangement with Delacorte Press

Interior illustration by Laura Hartman Maestro

Printed in the United States of America

March 1999

10 9 8 7 6 5 4 3 2 1

OPM

For Steven, of course

Ari carefully pressed open the crisp pages of *The Weekly Comet* and sank her teeth into a tuna-and-potato-chip sandwich. It was Saturday, her favorite day, because there were no lunch monitors around to swipe her newspaper and no need to worry about other kids' sodas spilling over the front-page headline: "Amazing Slug Sings 'Star-Spangled Banner.'" Ari smiled. Here at the kitchen table, she could linger in the wonderland of smiling celebrities, psychic predictions, and dim photos of aliens that looked suspiciously like gerbils wearing sunglasses.

But no. Lydia was still home. As soon as Ari heard her older sister galloping down the stairs, she leaned over her newspaper and tried to hide it with one arm. Drats. Even her own kitchen wasn't safe anymore.

The moment she walked in, Lydia noticed the newspaper and shot Ari a look of pure disgust. "Ulgh, not another one!" moaned Lydia, and she headed straight for the bananas on the table and snapped one off the bunch. Putting on a nasal British voice, she spoke into the banana microphone, her frizzy red hair bouncing as she slowly paced the kitchen floor:

"WELCOME TO *LIFESTYLES OF THE SHORT AND STUPID.* TODAY WE VISIT THE DEMENTED LIFE OF ARIADNE SPIRE, A PATHETIC ELEVEN-YEAR-OLD WHO THROWS AWAY A SMALL FORTUNE ON COMIC BOOKS, SUPERMARKET TABLOIDS, AND GOSSIP MAGAZINES. HERE IN HER HUMBLE SUBURBAN HOME, ARIADNE SPENDS COUNTLESS HOURS ALONE IN HER ROOM READING—AND REREADING—THIS OUTRAGEOUS JUNK. ASTONISHING? ABSOLUTELY. YET IT'S ALL PITIFULLY TRUE!" She dropped the accent and slapped the banana down on the table. "You really are pitiful, y'know that? I mean, it's not like your life has anything to do with the people in those magazines. It's totally irrelevant."

Ari's heart pumped fast. She wasn't sure what *irrelevant* meant, only that it was one of those big words Lydia used to make Ari feel, well, short and stupid. Ari nervously nibbled the end of her braid and tossed it back over her shoulder. Then she took

2

another enormous bite of her sandwich and turned back to her newspaper. Lydia was rummaging through the freezer. Maybe now she'd let Ari eat in peace.

"All right, hairball, where's the last Fudgsicle? It was here yesterday." Lydia turned around with her hand on her hip. "You ate that last Fudgsicle, didn't you?"

"You mean the one with your name engraved on it?" Ari pushed her purple glasses up on her nose and swallowed. "It's lo-o-ng gone. How 'bout a snot-sicle instead? There may still be one left."

Lydia shook her head in disgust. "That is so gross."

"Thank you," Ari replied. "It's the latest addition to the *Danny Ryder–Ari Spire Gross-Out Dictionary*."

"You guys are incredibly warped."

"You're too kind," said Ari, smiling at the thought of Danny and their collection of disgusting nouns.

"Even if he is your best friend," said Lydia, "I, for one, don't think it's such a tragedy he's moving. You two have arrested development."

"Danny's never been arrested," muttered Ari.

Lydia slammed the freezer door and found a bag of cookies. "Arrested development doesn't mean you go to *jail*, stupid. It means you've stopped growing up. You two act like little kids. You know what your problem is?" Ari put her hands over her ears. "*Your* problem is that you don't want to grow up." Ari wagged her head back and forth as she began singing "I Won't Grow Up" from *Peter Pan*. She cut her song short and flashed Lydia an obnoxious grin. Lydia rolled her eyes.

"So what's the junk-of-the-month you two are sending away for now?" Lydia was slowly pulling apart a Fig Newton, and as she moved closer to the table, Ari leaned further over her newspaper to protect it. "Crystal balls that turn out to be plastic marbles? Or how about the Gypsy Fortune-teller who charged a *fortune* for her predictions? Hah!" Lydia popped half the cookie into her mouth, and as she chewed, her eyes and mouth pinched into a serious expression. "I mean it, Ari, do you know how many *good* causes you could've helped with the money you've spent on this trash?" Ari dropped her chin into her hands, readying herself for the lecture. "Right now," said Lydia, "you and Danny could do so much for Waldo and Simone."

"Waldo and Simone?"

"A couple of walruses in the Arctic with a rare skin disease. If we could raise the money to help—"

"Walruses," Ari echoed. She turned a page, but Lydia suddenly swooped up the newspaper.

"Hey!—"

"All right, hairball, let's see what's the earthshaking news in here," said Lydia. "Oh my God, stop the

4

presses! Drop everything! Forget global warming—'*You* could fly to Hollywood and meet the *gorgeous, glamorous* stars of *Household Hunks*!'" Lydia pressed the newspaper to her chest and began to swoon. "Oh my God . . . I think I'm gonna faint!" She tried to catch Ari's eye, but Ari pretended to be absorbed in the memo on the refrigerator. As her eyes traced the loopdy-loops of her mother's handwriting, Lydia rolled the newspaper tightly in her hands and began pacing again.

"Y'know what really happens, Ari? They've got this publicity person, okay? And he says, 'Hey, guys, here's the kid from back East who won our contest. How 'bout a shot of the kid with one of our gorgeous stars?' Then one of the Household Hunks, who couldn't care *less* about you, puts his arms around your shoulders, and *click!* they've got their picture for their magazine. Then the publicity person says, 'Okay, get 'er outta here.' And you're on your way home." Lydia snorted. "A sucker born every minute. That's you. *And* Danny." She let the newspaper drop to the floor. Then, snatching up the bag of Fig Newtons, Lydia and her bouncing, frizzy red hair strode out of the kitchen.

Ari grabbed her newspaper and smoothed down the creases Lydia had inflicted. "Go kiss a walrus!" she yelled. Drats. She knew she'd think of a much better comeback hours later. But by then, who'd

5

care? Lately she'd been thinking about starting an *Insults for Lydia* book so that she could be ready with a good supply. Or maybe there was already a list out there you could send away for. Ari sat back in her chair, lost in the happy thought of a booklet chock-full of zingers arriving in the mail. Then she could really get back at Lydia, Miss I'm-fifteen-so-I-know-everything. Lydia was much more fun at fourteen, thought Ari. Then she turned fifteen, and *bam!* She changed into Miss World Crisis and spent all her time with some serious group at school that planned to save the rain forests and protect the animals. As far as Ari could tell, all these kids really did was sit around, eat Doritos, and gossip, while Lydia yelled: "Peeeepull! C'mon!" Talk about your waste of time.

Ari took a final bite of her sandwich, followed by two big slugs of chocolate milk to wash away the tuna breath. Then she ran up to her room and got ready to go over to Danny's house at the end of the block. For the past nine months they'd been working on a gum-wrapper chain that would eventually reach between their two houses. They were working hard to make it into *The Guinness Book of World Records* for the longest gum-wrapper chain ever made. So far, Ari's part of the chain went from her room, down the stairs, along the front hallway, out the door, and all the way to the sidewalk.

Ari and Danny had been friends since nursery school, not counting the brief time in second grade when Danny thought all girls had cooties. And though it was never made an official rule, Ari and Danny rarely spoke to each other in school. Some kids just wouldn't understand. So they waited till they crossed Water Street and started up the shady hill of Highland Avenue. Then they felt free to talk, trade comic books at each other's houses, and send away for secret stuff.

Ari liked being with Danny because he was the only other kid she'd ever known who loved old movies. They would take turns watching them at each other's houses, and sometimes pooled their money at the video store. But lately, Ari noticed they were having a hard time agreeing on what to watch. Danny had gotten hooked on John Wayne Westerns and some of the Humphrey Bogart films. Bo-ring, thought Ari. She wished he still liked the old musicals best. Her favorite was *The Wizard of Oz*. She knew the whole film by heart—except for one part. When the Wicked Witch's guards marched around her castle, were they saying: (a) "Oh, *we* don't love *no* one," (b) *"Oh* Wee-oh, the *old* one," or (c) "Or-E-os, they're *all* right"? It drove Ari nuts.

Ari stood in front of her dresser and ran her tongue over her teeth to check for any lingering scraps of food. Then she took off her glasses. Tilting

7

her head, she pretended to dab perfume on either side of her neck, and in her best movie-star whisper confided to the audience in the mirror: "Sapphire Moon. Because it suits me." For a moment Ari stared at herself. Then she pulled open her sock drawer and reached in back for the piece of paper that would change her life. "Now You Can Have the Irresistible and Infamous Violet Eyes of Movie Legend Ruby Lockheart!!!" read the tiny black-and-white ad. "Send Today for Exciting Information on Violet-Colored Contact Lenses with Our UNIQUE and EXCLUSIVE MICRO SPARKLE POINTS that put the STARS IN *YOUR* EYES!!!" Ari's heart always raced with excitement when she read this ad.

She squatted down and reached into the bottom of her sweater drawer. Under her sweaters was an old knit hat where she'd been quietly stashing part of her allowance. Over the months the hat had grown heavy and stretched out from her diligent saving, and she could almost see the day when she would shed this boring old familiar Ari skin and emerge the glamorous Ariadne, with points of light shooting out from her violet eyes. She dug her fingers into her pocket and dropped two quarters into the hat.

Lydia may know how to save walruses and change the world, thought Ari, but I know how to change my life to make it magical. Just like Ariadne

8

in her book of Greek myths, Ariadne Spire believed that one day something extraordinary would happen to her. It just had to. She pushed her purple glasses back onto her face and pulled on her weekend uniform: a blue hooded sweatshirt and a neon-orange baseball cap.

"I'm going!" she yelled. On her way out, she checked the mailbox. Nothing. Then she remembered that Sinbad's Genuine Magic Potion Kit would be coming to Danny's house, not hers. Without mail to look forward to, life was as gray as the stretch between Valentine's Day and Easter Sunday. True excitement, Ari knew, was a thick, wrinkled orange-yellow package with lots of postage and your name on it. And within the smooth newsprint pages of *Aladdin's Catalog of Wonders* was the promise of kits (Ari's favorite word was *kit*) and pamphlets and all kinds of amazing things that could make your life extraordinary. Something special would happen to her, she knew, just by her saving those box tops and clipping those little coupons and checking "Yes! I'll Send Today!" She slammed down the mailbox cover and resolved to send away for something new before the day was done.

Chapter 2

Ari knew Danny was in a foul mood as soon as he opened the door. He was still in sweatpants, and his pale face was dry and crusty from sleep.

"Did it come yet?" Ari asked, pushing her way into the house. Danny stumbled back a step.

"Huh?" He ran his fingers quickly through his thick brown hair, then wiped the back of his hand across his mouth.

"The magic-potion kit! Remember? *Aladdin's Catalog of Wonders*, page forty-three?" Danny's mouth was open, like a little kid watching TV.

He blinked and croaked, barely moving his lips, "Oh, yeah. I mean, no—it didn't come yet." He turned and started up the stairs. "C'mon up," he mumbled, and Ari followed him two steps at a time up the creaky staircase with the worn brown carpeting. She loved Danny's dark, rambling house; its smell of dried apricots and old upholstery always gave her a safe, cozy feeling.

"You have frozen pizza again for breakfast?" she asked.

"Nah—all out," he replied. "Felt more like a fish-stick-and-Fudgsicle kind of morning, anyway." Ari gulped. She was used to the idea that Danny's mother let him eat whatever he wanted, as long as he worked in the four basic food groups. But some of his combinations made her wince.

"Where's your mom?"

"Dragged Frank furniture shopping with her. Ulgh."

"Ulgh," echoed Ari. By the time they reached the upstairs, Danny seemed more awake, and he jumped for the first metal bar stuck high overhead in the hallway near his room. Ari automatically stepped back, giving him room to hoist himself up and perform a double flip over the bar. He landed with a firm thump and, like an Olympian, dramatically thrust his arms straight up over his head.

"Mmm—I give it a seven point five," Ari said.

"Agghh!" yelled Danny, and ran into his room, diving facedown onto his bed. Then he sat up and started picking the lint out from between his toes.

"You're incredibly weird today," said Ari. "What's up?"

"I dunno. This moving stuff stinks," Danny grumbled. "I'm supposed to spend the day cleaning my closet and throw out any junk I don't want to take to the new house."

Ari looked around Danny's messy room. "One day isn't enough for that," she said. Danny wrinkled his mouth in agreement.

"And right in the middle of moving and my mom getting married, she suddenly decides to switch from Carefree to Trident! You can't make a chain with those puny wrappers—sheesh!"

"Well, maybe Frank likes Trident better. Why don't you ask her to switch back? And don't pick your toes in front of me. It's gross."

"I did ask her! She said she would, as soon as she finished the pack. And of course it's one of those packs with five jillion pieces that'll probably last till I'm her age. Do you really think she switched to Trident 'cause of Frank?"

"Never know. Remember, they're in that gushy about-to-get-remarried stage. Anything's possible." Ari walked around his bed to take a closer look at the fishbowl on the night table. The bowl was full of foggy water and something else. It looked like drifting pieces of lint. Ari squinted at the tiny floating shapes. "What's in there?" she asked, glancing at Danny's toe pickings, then back at the foggy water.

"Those," said Danny majestically, "are Sea Monkeys. Sea Monkeys! Do *you* see monkeys?" Ari turned and smiled at him. "Remember when I told you I'd sent away for them? I spent a whole month's allowance on this mega–rip-off. I bought the bowl, the plants, the treasure chest—everything. I figured I was finally gonna have a pet my mother would let me keep. And what'd I get? Little smiling monkeys doing neat tricks?"

Ari searched the bowl for some sign of amusing activity. Nope.

"Hey, wait a minute!" she exclaimed. "Where's the one wearing the little crown?" Danny threw his pillow at her. "I mean it," she said, laughing. "There's *always* one with a crown. Now I know what's wrong with this setup—they didn't send you the King of the Sea Monkeys. Demand a refund!"

"Shut up," said Danny. He bounced off his bed and peered into the bowl. "Y'know what those are? Brine shrimp!"

Ari looked at him, puzzled. "What?"

"They're tiny crustaceans that look like—like fingernail clippings," Danny said. "They float around in there all curled up until they just get bored and die." Ari started nibbling on the end of her braid. Looking at Danny's pale morning profile, she could see he was genuinely disappointed.

"Maybe these aren't the real Sea Monkeys," she offered. "I think you got some cheapo brand by mistake."

"I really thought I was going to have a pet," Danny said quietly.

Ari jumped up, grabbed the chin-up bar at the top of his doorway, and began to swing back and forth.

"Hey, guess what?" she said cheerily. "There's actually a movie playing at the Capital that we don't need our parents to take us to!"

"Oh, right," said Danny glumly. "What is it—*Needle Nerds from Neptune?*"

"No!" Ari let go of the bar and watched Danny as he gently sprinkled Sea Monkey food into the fishbowl. With his other hand he lightly tapped the glass, beckoning the floating apostrophes to perform.

"Yeah, so what's the movie?" Danny grumbled.

Ari made her I'm-in-a-movie face by widening her eyes and raising her eyebrows. She started sashaying about the room, singing with an English accent: " 'Up in a balloon, boys, up in a balloon.' " She suddenly stopped her little jig and put her hands out, pausing for the answer. Danny's face lit up.

"Gaslight!" he yelled. "It's *Gaslight*? Are you kidding me? *Gaslight*?"

"Yep! Once again, iiiiiitttt's—revival week at the Capital!" *Gaslight* was their favorite chiller. It was about a man who makes his wife think she's going crazy.

Ari stuck her hands deep into her pockets and rocked on her heels. "So whaddya say, pardner? Wanna mosey on down to the old movie house, rustle up some popcorn, and take in a flick?" Danny was smiling now.

"Okay, pardner," he answered. "Time to head for the tall and uncut."

"I'll saddle up the horses," said Ari, starting out of his room.

"Wait!" yelled Danny. "Y'wanna see something?" He lunged across his bed and pulled out a shoe box from underneath. Brushing off the dustballs, he opened it and held it out to Ari. Inside was a collection of cardboard strips: box tops for the miniature Swiss Army knife Danny was saving for.

"There's fourteen of those li'l beauties in there."

Ari's eyebrows went up. "You've sure gone through a lot of Swiss oatmeal," she said, impressed.

Danny nodded. "Only six more boxes and that Swiss Mini Deluxe is mine!" He slapped the shoe box lid down as though too much air might make the box tops inside disappear. Ari always teased him that *Swiss Mini Deluxe* sounded more like a weeny little cheeseburger than a knife, but Danny never laughed. Getting that pocketknife meant a lot to him.

"Does it really come with a flashlight and a fishing line?"

"You bet it does, shweethaht," he said in his Humphrey Bogart voice.

Turning to leave, Ari grabbed an old sneaker from the floor and threw it at his head. "I *told* you not to call me that!" She ran out, laughing. The sneaker came flying back out and landed in one of the many laundry baskets lined up in the hallway.

A minute later, Danny galumphed past Ari on the stairs.

"And this time," he announced, "we don't blow all our money on peppermint patties. Those things are gross."

"Not as gross as Milk Duds."

"Hey, you can't say anything bad about Milk Duds—they reign supreme!"

"I hate Milk Duds!" Ari yelled to the ceiling. "They cement themselves to your teeth and stab you with their little caramel points! They're duds—get it? Milk *Duds*! It's peppermint patty time, ole buddy, ole pal."

Outside Danny's house, they checked the mailbox. Empty. "I can't wait till that magic-potion kit comes," said Ari. "You'll see. It'll change our lives forever!"

Danny looked doubtful. "Right. Then maybe I won't have to move."

Ari studied him for a moment. "Well, you never know." She shrugged and smiled weakly. Then she tapped him on the shoulder. "C'mon, race ya. Ready-set-go-you're-too-slow!" And they both jumped away from the mailbox and sped down the hill.

Chapter

3

"Sit down, sit down, you're rocking the boat!" chanted Mrs. Atwood, standing at the front of the classroom. Ari's fifth-grade class had just returned from gym. They were loud and sweaty, their faces still red. Peter Martindale pushed Ari on the way to his desk.

"Hey, move your Ari-odd-knees!" he huffed.

"Shut up, Fartindale," she shot back. Peter's curls were still dripping from when he had dunked his whole head into the water fountain. Rocking back and forth in his chair, he sang out like a teacher: "Is *everyone* here today? Ari-*odd*-knee? Ari-*odd*-knee Spire? Where *are* you?" Some of the other boys laughed.

It was never easy being an Ariadne. No one could pronounce this name from Greek mythology. It

18

wasn't well known, like *Mercury* or *Pandora*, and she was always having to correct people: No, it's Ar-ee-AD-nee. Ari liked it, but calling herself Ariadne would be like prancing into school wearing a large, fancy hat. It wouldn't matter that the hat was beautiful; she would still feel ridiculous. So she tried on the name when no one was looking, on cold mornings when she could write her name with her finger on the window and watch it quickly drip away, or in the margins of her paper, where among the doodles she scribbled *Ariadne* in every possible handwriting and studied each one, as if they had different personalities.

Mrs. Atwood flicked the lights off and on. The room rumbled with the sounds of slamming desks and kids skidding into their chairs.

"Please find your seats—qui-et-ly," said Mrs. Atwood. Her voice was clear and soft. She never had to yell. As she stood by the door, with her hands on her hips, and her shapely dark eyebrows raised, Mrs. Atwood's silence was far more powerful than any yelling. Ari loved watching her teacher's spellbinding silence at work. It was scary and thrilling at the same time; she was sure Mrs. Atwood possessed magic powers. Ari loved the way her teacher's face shifted from moment to moment: laughter, concern, wonder, disapproval, excitement, impatience—and always with the eyebrows arched.

I bet those eyebrows just collapse on the weekend, thought Ari.

Mrs. Atwood took one hand off her hip to run her fingers through the left side of her wavy salt-and-pepper hair. She always did this when the class acted up. It was as though Mrs. Atwood drew strength from some power source stashed in the left side of her hair. She looked at Peter.

"Mr. Martindale," Mrs. Atwood said slowly, emphasizing each syllable, "would you please do us all a kindness by settling yourself down."

"Mr. Martindale" was red in the face and having a hard time containing his laughter. At last, he burst. "We had a substitute in gym and when she took attendance she called out 'Ari-odd-knee!'" Muffled tittering could be heard throughout the class. Ari dug her pencil hard into her book cover, pretending it was Peter's face. As Mrs. Atwood walked over to Peter's desk, the large metal beads of her necklace jangled softly on her bosom.

"And you find this amusing?" Mrs. Atwood lowered her chin into the soft flesh beneath it and widened her green eyes. The dark eyeliner extended past the corners of her eyes, and, staring straight at Peter, she was like an owl sizing up a juicy little mouse. The class was so quiet that they could hear the hum of the fluorescent lights above. Peter Martindale stopped laughing and wiggled in his seat. He shrugged. He squirmed. He slumped down in his chair. His face was still red, but now it was from embarrassment.

"I thought they covered name-calling and teasing in the first grade, Peter. Perhaps you need a little review." He looked scared. Ari pursed her lips in satisfaction. Mrs. Atwood glanced at Ari, then back at Peter. "Besides, I think Ariadne is a beautiful name." Ari blushed.

Mrs. Atwood looked back at Ari with one eyebrow arched, and Ari smiled, hoping her teacher could read her thoughts: Thanks, Atwood. The goddess Athena couldn't have done better.

Mrs. Atwood's long pleated skirt swooshed with authority as she strolled back to her desk and put on her glasses.

"All right, people. Listen up." She opened the folded paper in her hand. "Proclamation from the queen. It seems that next month we'll be observing National Dental Hygiene Week. You're all to submit posters for the school contest. Naturally, the posters should say something about caring for your teeth." A hand shot up.

"What's the prize?"

"A full set of dentures!" a voice shouted from the back of the room. Mrs. Atwood laughed.

"What's the prize? Hmm, I'm not sure, but it says here that the winning posters from each grade will

21

be displayed in the glass case downstairs. You should work on them at home and bring them in to school next month."

Mrs. Atwood put down the paper and rubbed her hands together. "All right, let's take out our social studies books, and would the book monitor please distribute the dictionaries. I want to continue our explication of the Pledge of Allegiance. I think last time we clarified that it is not 'for witches stands' but 'for which it stands.'" The class laughed, and Ari smiled, remembering how proud she had been in kindergarten to learn that her own sister's name was in the daily pledge: ". . . with Lydia and justice for all."

Suddenly Ari felt a note pressed into her hand. Her heartbeat accelerated to a billion miles an hour. Notes were rarely good news when they came from the direction of Martina Wallhoffer. Martina was the kind who fooled grown-ups into thinking she woudn't hurt a fly. But the kids knew different. Not only would Martina Wallhoffer yank the wings right off the fly, she'd manage to convince you that the fly deserved it.

Once, in the second grade, Holly Waters had sneezed so hard that she had wet her pants and had to wait in the nurse's office for her mother to bring her fresh underwear. Martina never let her forget it. Even in third grade Martina would taunt her in front of other kids: "Hey, did you know that Holly *Waters* the whole classroom?" But then when someone made fun of Holly's lunch box, who put her arm around her and acted like her big sister? Martina. You just couldn't figure her out.

Martina was also the supreme authority on the correct things to like and dislike. After being in the same class for three months, Ari knew the Martina manifesto by heart. She knew that lilac and magenta were the very *best* of all possible colors, that peppermint-stick ice cream and lime sherbet were the only really *good* flavors, that *Household Hunks* and *Dancing for Dollars* were *the* TV shows to watch, and that boys secretly liked to be brushed on the back of their hands with indelible ink. In fact, there didn't seem to be any aspect of fifth-grade life that Martina didn't have a ruling on. For Ari, there was something strangely attractive about that.

Ari opened up the folded pink paper below the horizon of her desk and tried not to inhale the paper's sickly sweet aroma: cheery cherry. The dreaded words hit her like a bowling ball: "I'm mad at you. Your almost X-Friend, Martina." Without having to look, Martina knew when the note had been read, and slowly turned to glare at Ari. Martina narrowed her squinty brown eyes and sucked in her lips. That was it. Then she turned back to her work, gripping her pink pen with the heart eraser.

Ari looked around the classroom for someone to rescue her. But Danny was in the other fifth-grade class and everyone else was safely absorbed in their work, defining the word *indivisible*. Hannah Swensen, the smartest kid in the fifth grade, had already finished and was looking around for something to do besides sweep her stringy hair out of her face a hundred times. Ari took the end of her own hair into her hand and began chewing on the tip of her braid. Being Martina's X-Friend was about the worst thing that could happen to a person. Martina had ways of knowing what could really humiliate someone, and it was generally believed that one should just pack up and move to another planet rather than endure being Martina's X-Friend.

Out of the corner of her eye, Ari watched the Dingles, Bethany and Brianna. They stood at the pencil sharpener, grinding their pencils down to nubs while holding one of their secret conferences. The identical twins were the quietest girls in the fifth grade, and they almost never smiled. They stayed together and had quiet conversations that never included anyone else. No one paid much attention to them, and they seemed to like it that way.

Those two are probably spies working undercover, thought Ari. Lucky them. Why couldn't Martina just ignore her the way she ignored the Dingles? Why couldn't Ari blend into the gray-green walls of the classroom the way those twins did?

Ari looked across the room at Clarinda Pallaster. Another one Martina didn't touch. Clarinda took ballet lessons in Boston and danced in *The Nutcracker* at Christmastime. She was small and black, with shiny hair that was always pulled into a bun. She never slouched, but sat straight up, shoulders back, the way Ari's mother always said people should sit. Martina and her little group had tried to find her guilty of being stuck-up but had failed. Clarinda was polite and always busy after school. Martina might have been queen of the playground, but Clarinda performed on a much bigger stage. That alone made her untouchable.

Then there's me, thought Ari, stuck somewhere in between Clarinda and the Dingles. That made her fair game for Martina. Suddenly Ari was aware of someone hovering over her. She looked up. It was Mrs. Atwood and her owl eyes.

"Anything interesting out there in Never-Never Land?" she asked. Ari yanked her hair out of her mouth, crushed the notepaper in her hand, and went back to work.

When the class lined up for dismissal, Ari managed to sidle up to Martina.

"Why are you mad at me?" said Ari. Martina

didn't take her eyes off the head in front of her. It was part of her technique. "Martina, *answer* me. Why did you write that you were mad at me?" It was hard at this point not to seem desperate, which was exactly what Martina wanted. Finally Martina turned around. Her overlapping front teeth bit her lower lip in exasperation.

"Because," she said, as though she were pointing out the obvious, "you didn't sit next to me in music. I sent you a note about it on Friday." Ari felt slightly ill.

"I'm sorry," she said quickly. "I forgot—I thought you wanted to sit with Tara like you always do." Martina stared ahead, considering this excuse. Ari waited for the verdict.

"We-e-e-ll," Martina said, squinting her eyes into tiny slits, "hmm. Okay—I forgive you." She didn't smile, but Ari felt limp with relief.

"By the way," said Martina, looking Ari up and down, "doesn't your mother ever take you shopping? You always wear the same thing." Ari looked down at her favorite purple jeans and touched the neck of her shirt. It was a plain white turtleneck. When she was with Danny, she'd roll the neck all the way up till it covered her nose and only her glasses stuck out. Then he would call her Bugwoman and she would chase him, threatening to cover him with bug slime. Martina would definitely call it a baby game and tease her about it till the day she died, if she ever found out.

"I don't always wear the same thing. I just like this outfit, that's all." Though Ari really didn't think too much about clothes, she wished that at this moment she could fold tabs around her body like a paper doll and instantly be covered in the kind of clothes Martina would approve of. Ari adjusted her glasses. This gesture always gave her confidence.

Martina flattened her lips, and her eyes traveled up and down Ari's body as she shook her head slowly: the official "boy, are you weird" look.

"Well, you could've at least worn your hair down like me," said Martina.

The heavy school doors opened with their familiar *clunk-squeak*, letting in a whoosh of raw November air.

Ari gave a hard yank on her stuck jacket zipper and, to show her appreciation for being forgiven, said, "You're right, Martina. I should try wearing my hair down. Your hair always looks so great." And she dashed out into the schoolyard, eager to get to Danny's house and play their favorite game.

Chapter

4

They called it Quest for Survival. No one else knew about their game, but they had been playing it since they were six. Over the years, they had changed the name. At first it was called Hansel and Gretel, then Lost in the Woods. By fourth grade they named it Quest for Survival, which made it sound more dangerous. Some things never changed, though. The game always began with Ari and Danny being sent away because their parents could no longer afford to keep them. Their only food was one slice of American cheese and one piece of white bread apiece, and it had to last for days. Then they had to find shelter and food and survive all the dangers that lay ahead.

"I see a cave!" shouted Danny, pointing to a brambly hedge that had lost all its leaves. "There's lots of berries right near it. I'm going to check it out and see if we can take shelter there."

"Are you nuts? Don't you know what's in that cave?"

"No. What?"

"The Cyclops!"

"So what? Who are they?"

"They're not a *they*, they're an *it*. And *it* is a *huge* monster with one *huge* eye right in the middle—like this—*boing!* And I hate to tell you this, but the Cyclops is no vegetarian. You walk in there, and you're shrimp cocktail." Danny scowled at her, and Ari rolled her eyes.

"I didn't mean shrimp like you're shrimpy," she sighed. Danny was smaller than most of the boys in the fifth grade and would jump anyone who made fun of him.

"I don't believe there's any Cyklutz in there," he grumbled.

"All right, all right, if you insist. But I'm not going to save you again this time. I'm going to look for some food for our supper."

"What're you talking about, saving me? You never saved me."

"Oh, yeah? What about last week when you were trapped in the labyrinth with the Minotaur? Who saved you from that monster, mister? None other than Ariadne, the fearless princess of Crete!" Ari laughed as she stretched up her arms in victory. Having a father who taught ancient history and literature gave her a headful of Greek myths and legends to play out with Danny.

Danny ignored Ari's victory dance. "You can go save someone else from the Minotaur," he said. "I'm going Cyclops hunting!" And he turned three perfect cartwheels, then sprinted away.

Ari headed off in the opposite direction. After filling her pockets with berries from the bushes in front of the house, she started back toward the swings. Danny was groaning and limping toward her with one pant leg rolled up and his hand on his knee.

"What happened?" she yelled, running toward him. His thin face was squeezed in pain, and his leg appeared to be bloodied.

"Inside the cave," he said. His voice was hoarse. "The Cyclops. It missed me by *this* much," and he showed her a slice of air between his fingers. Then he collapsed on the grass. Ari nodded seriously as she examined the spots of dark red berries he'd smooshed to look like blood.

"This looks pretty bad," she said, lifting Danny's hand off his blood-red knee.

"We've gotta go back in that cave and kill it," sighed Danny. "It's hungry, and I think we're the first meat it's sniffed in days!" Ari ran to the outside faucet that hooked up to the sprinkler in summertime. There was a small, dirty plastic sand bucket nearby, which she filled with water. Then she picked up some large brown leaves from the ground and headed back toward Danny.

The clouds hung low and gray, and Ari shivered as the sharp autumn wind cut through her jacket. She bent down next to Danny and wrapped the wet brown leaves around his leg. "Yow! That's cold!" he screamed. Carefully Ari rolled down his pant leg and supported him as he limped over to the back steps. They sat down and pulled out their bread and cheese from a hole in one of the steps.

"We need to get some long sticks and sharpen the ends till they're really pointy," Ari said, taking mouse-sized bites from the bread. "Then we lunge at the Cyclops's one eye and *squirt*—it's blinded! Did you bring your knife?"

Danny's body sagged, and his look of mock pain was replaced with bug-eyed exasperation. "You *know* I still don't have enough box tops for the knife!"

Ari looked back at him, irritated. "I'm not talking about *that* knife, I just meant a *pretend* kni—"

"Dan-ny!" A voice shouted from inside the house. They both looked up and saw the shadowy figure of Danny's mother behind the screen door.

"Ari, your mom called and wants you home." Danny and Ari were so used to one of their mothers interrupting that they almost considered it part of the game.

"Righto!" Ari yelled back. Then they both shoved more bread and cheese into their mouths.

"And Danny!" his mother shouted. "You need to come in *now* and do something about your room! I mean it!"

"I'd rather face a Cyclops," Danny mumbled through his mouthful of food.

"Mmm," answered Ari. "I don't blame you. What's with her? Your mom used to be so nice and smiley all the time. But I don't know, lately she's turned into a—a Momotaur—half Mom, half monster!"

"Yeah." Danny laughed. "Sometimes." He rolled a small piece of bread into a ball. "I think she's got a bad case of weddingitis."

"And movingitis?" said Ari.

Danny popped the bread ball into his mouth. "Yeah, she's a nervous wreck 'cause of everything that's going on. I'll be glad when this is all over." Danny looked uneasily at Ari, then threw the bread ball high into the air and tilted his head way back to catch it.

Ari swallowed the last of her cheese. "Well, I better break camp and head for the hills," she said, brushing the crumbs from her pants. "Next time, I'll bring a good paring knife for sharpening our sticks. That Cyclops won't have a chance against the two of us."

After supper Ari worked on her poster for Dental Hygiene Week. When her mother came into the kitchen, she looked over Ari's shoulder at the rough sketch on the table and read: " 'Teeth Don't Die— You Kill Them! Brush!' A bit melodramatic, isn't it?" said her mother quietly.

Ari studied the pad. "Well, it's supposed to have punch. That's what our teacher said. She said, 'Make sure your slogans have plenty of punch.' I thought I'd show a bunch of teeth all lined up to look like little gravestones." Ari's mother widened her eyes and cocked her head. Ari knew this was her mother's way of not hurting her feelings when she thought her ideas stank.

"It certainly is original," her mother offered, and went to the stove to stir a big vat of chili. Her mother was stockpiling food for the next few weeks. She always did this when there was a new show at the art gallery where she worked. Ari pushed her chair out and stood up straight.

"Well, that's what they want—originality. I don't want to do the same old smiling Mr. Happy Tooth with his sidekick, Miss Toothpaste. That's old hat, Mom," Ari said loudly. "Besides, what's wrong with being original? How am I supposed to win if I don't do something original?"

Mrs. Spire's shoulders sagged. "Ari, you don't have to be so touchy. I never said you should be 'old hat.' I don't think you could be old hat if you tried." Her mother turned back to her chili, and Ari watched her for a moment, sorry that she had snapped at her mother, but not sorry enough to say so.

Mrs. Spire worked at an art gallery three days during the week and on Saturdays. On her days home, she lived in old sweats and cooked enough food to last till the twenty-third century. But when she worked at the gallery, she was transformed into someone glamorous and fast-talking. At the end of the day, she collapsed on the sofa like a movie star, with her high heels kicked off and a glass of wine in her hand. To Ari, she was like the comic-book heroes who lived a secret second life.

"Mom . . ." Ari didn't know how to apologize to her parents anymore. "Could Danny come for supper this week? There aren't going to be too many more chances."

"Ari, he's not exactly moving to the moon, y'know. You can still visit each other."

"I know, but it's not going to be the same. I don't see why Frank can't just move into Danny's old house after he and Danny's mother get married. It's not fair. Why should Danny have to move? Frank should just bring his stuff to Danny's house."

"It isn't that simple, Ari. This isn't a *dog* you bring home to live with you." Ari's mother had a way of pronouncing certain words as though she were pumping blood into them. When an ordinary word like *dog* came out of her mother's mouth, Ari could really sense a big, smelly dog. "Danny and his mom are starting a new *life* with Frank."

"But there was nothing wrong with Danny's old life! He liked his life. *I* liked his life. Danny's the one being treated like a dog, if you ask me."

"Ari," Mrs. Spire said sharply, "this is hard for you to see right now, but it's all going to be fine— even for Danny."

"Yeah, but what about for me?" fumed Ari. She slapped her notebook against her side and stomped out of the room.

To make herself feel better, she shoved a tape into her cassette player and settled into her reading niche for a visit with her comics and movie magazines.

As the overture to *Peter Pan* filled her room, she felt the world melt away. It was perfect here on the floor of her room, snuggled in between her bed and bookcase. The space was so small that Ari had to crouch with her legs bent and the soft, worn pages of *Aladdin's Catalog of Wonders* resting on her knees. She liked the way it brought her right up close to the promises of the cramped advertisements in tiny black newsprint. This gap she had arranged in the furniture also worked its magic in making the rest of the house disappear, so that the whole world shrank down to an enchanted three feet of space—just enough room for Ari, her comic-book friends, and all the wonderful things you could send for.

Nestled in the magazine's landscape of whoopee cushions and Sea Monkeys was a world of magic. No Danny moving away and no Martina Wallhoffers. But just staring at the ads wouldn't change anything. She would have to find something out there that would transform her, make her as untouchable as Clarinda and the Dingles. Ari laughed to herself. Imagine, the Dingles extraordinary! But they were. Twins always were. She put down the catalog and pulled out the latest edition of *The Weekly Comet*. "Teen Discovers Life-Saving Cures of Miracle Onion Dip," read the sensational headline.

What was sensational about Ari Spire? She lived in a simple red house on a shady block with an ordinary mom, an ordinary dad, and an ordinary sister. Ari sang along with the tape: "Just *think* of lovely *things*, and your *heart* will fly on *wings* for*ever* in never-*never land*!" Ari turned a page: "Discover the Exciting Career That's Right for You!" She grabbed a pen. As she circled her responses to the questions, she imagined herself a few years from now. She was waving to her family from the steps of a roaring airplane before being whisked away to Hollywood, where she would become manager to the stars or maybe run a model agency. It would be like a movie, with music in the background—sad, but at the same time exhilarating.

Ari suddenly dropped the paper, disgusted.

Why did she ache to live in those old movie plots, where every moment was experienced so intensely, and so musically? Why wasn't it enough just to be on the Brink of Adolescence? That was what the school nurse had called it the day she had herded the girls into the library and exposed the plot to overturn their childhood. Martina had giggled and made a big show of it in front of the boys. As if it were the greatest thing. But for Ari, all this talk about Growing Up and the Wonderful Changes in You made her feel like the cartoon character Wile E. Coyote falling over the edge into the Grand Canyon of Adolescence with some lame Acme rocket strapped to her back. Ari chewed her braid thoughtfully. And of course, the engines are filled with nothing but marshmallow fluff, and *pff-fft!* Down I go. *Crash, smash, boom!* Th-th-that's all, folks!

Thinking of the Acme company reminded her of sending away, which reminded her of Danny and the ten gum wrappers she'd collected that day. She took them out of her pencil case as proof that Danny's moving away wouldn't change things. Their paper chain would always keep them connected. Sitting cross-legged on her bed, she began folding the wrappers into the paper links that would one day connect her house to Danny's.

Rip-fold-fold-connect. Rip-fold-fold-connect. With each new link, Ari felt herself moving further from the Brink and more toward Danny. Rip-fold-fold-connect. Rip-fold-fold-connect.

Chapter

5

"You've gotta come over this afternoon!" said Danny as their teams switched places. It was recess, and the fifth-graders were getting in the last of the kickball games before winter took over the playground. As Ari sauntered out to take second base, she kept turning around to keep her eyes on Peter Martindale. He looked ready to kick the brick-colored ball into her face.

"Can't come today," she muttered softly, without even looking at Danny. Then she tapped her front teeth. "I have to go to the dentist. I might need braces—yikes!"

Danny stooped down to tie his shoelace and spoke without looking up, as though they were secret agents. "Remember that magic-potion kit we sent away for?"

"It came?"

"Yeah—the other day. It looks good, too. I bet if we combined our magic powers from the potions with information from the Ouija board, we could do some really good magic." He looked up for the first time and nodded toward a small crowd of girls. "Maybe turn Wallhoffer into a cockroach or something!" Ari quickly looked around to make sure Martina hadn't heard him.

"C'mon, you guys!" Kevin Slater yelled. "Let's move it!"

"That sounds great," said Ari. "But I can't till tomorrow, okay?"

"Okay, okay," Danny muttered. He jumped onto his hands and walked upside down. "Yow! It's cold!" he yelled into the air, and bounced right back onto his feet.

"Show-off!" Ari said to herself, making her way to second base. She watched Danny as he was folded back into the group of sweaty fifth-grade boys. There didn't seem to be a Martina among them. Just an occasional stupid remark from someone like Peter; but then, that was usually taken care of by a quick, hard punch on the arm. Then it would be over and they would all be friends again. Maybe that's the secret, thought Ari. Maybe if the girls

40

punched each other in the arm once in a while, life would be a little easier.

Ari glanced over to the corner of the playground where Martina was holding court. As usual, she was surrounded by her loyal subjects, skinny Danielle and Tara, who towered over Martina but still did everything she said. Suddenly Ari noticed Martina looking over at her, and, afraid that she might have read her thoughts, she waved cheerfully. Just then the kickball came flying through the air, smacking Ari in the face.

A laughing Peter was galloping over to first base. "Nice going," he yelled, while Martina and her little group laughed.

When Ari's class went back to their room, their heads all turned to the word RELAX!!!!! written on the board. That single word covered the entire green chalkboard, followed by so many exclamation marks it looked like a chalk maniac had crept into the room during recess. Dazed, the class collapsed into their seats and looked to Mrs. Atwood for an explanation.

"Class," she said in a formal voice, "for the next hour we'll be working on these standardized tests." She held up an official-looking white booklet. It reminded Ari of the paper on doctors' examination tables. She pictured her whole class removing their clothes and folding them neatly on their chairs.

"I'm sure many of you are already familiar with these tests," said Mrs. Atwood. "We'll go over all the instructions together. Do you remember the other day I asked you to bring in two sharpened number two pencils?" The class sat as if they had been shot with a stun gun. "If any of you need to sharpen your pencils, please do so now."

Half the class jumped up and ran to the pencil sharpener by the window. The grinding noise and pushing at the sharpener made them feel like themselves again. But after all the pencils had been sharpened and the instructions explained, the formal feeling was back in the air. Ari sat stiffly at her desk.

Mrs. Atwood watched the large clock above the door. The second hand clicked—*ka-chunk*—to the twelve. Keeping her eyes on the clock, she said, "You may begin."

Ari quickly flipped through the pages to see how long the test was. At the bottom of one page there was a tiny drawing of a hand, palm up, inside a stop sign. It was going to be a long haul before she'd reach that little hand.

"Eyes on your own paper, Mr. Myers" was the only thing Mrs. Atwood said. Pencils twitched up and down, coloring in tiny ovals on the answer sheets.

With her head down, Ari looked over at Brian

Tucker writing with one pencil while busily munching on his extra one. He looked like a beaver working on an ear of corn. Munch, munch, munch. Ari's eyes were fixed on him turning the pencil and sinking his front teeth into a fresh space. She made a note to herself never to borrow a pencil from Brian. Then she sank her teeth into her own pencil. She examined her teeth marks. It was satisfying in its own peculiar way, but she just wasn't a pencil chewer.

Suddenly from the back of the room came a retching sound. Everyone in 5A was snapped out of their test-taking hypnosis. It was Clarinda Pallaster. She had thrown up right in the middle of section two. Mrs. Atwood hurried to her side.

"Are you all right?" she asked Clarinda, whose face was the color of weak chocolate milk. Clarinda nodded. "Why don't you go to the girls' room and wash your face. Then we'll go to the nurse's office. I'll get Mrs. Kane to come in." Clarinda rose carefully and walked out of the room as if in a trance.

All eyes were now on Mrs. Atwood as she approached Clarinda's test booklet. Her usual expression of wide-eyed surprise shifted to a cross between fear and disgust. Standing at one side of Clarinda's desk, she quickly slammed the booklet closed, as if that would make the vomit go away on its own. Instead, it made a kind of muffled splat, spurting out of the edges. A chorus of "Eeeeww" rose up on cue. Mrs. Atwood looked at her audience with her hands on her hips.

"Five more minutes for this section," she said. "I strongly suggest you get back to work."

Mrs. Atwood ran her hand through the left side of her hair several times as she made her way over to the intercom on the wall. She buzzed for the custodian and another teacher to cover her class, and soon Mrs. Kane from down the hall was sitting at Mrs. Atwood's desk with her arms crossed. Her eyes traveled over the classroom as though it were filled with sleeping tigers. The only break in the silence came when Kevin Slater fell off his chair and everyone laughed.

Ari knew the answer to the final question and eagerly colored in the last oval. Satisfied, she lifted her head and took a look around the room. She was one of the first ones done. Looking down at her answer sheet, she admired the zigzag pattern made by all the tiny dark ovals. It was like a line of ants crawling on her paper. Then panic struck. One blank oval was left over. Instead of cute little ants, Ari's paper looked like a sweater buttoned all wrong. With only a few minutes left, she would have to erase all her answers and move them down by one oval. Furiously she began erasing, whispering to herself:

"Thirty-one b, thirty d, (oh my God) twenty-nine a, twenty-eight b, (oh my God) twenty-seven c," and so on, while in another corner of her mind she was down on her hands and knees praying to Zeus that time wouldn't run out, that she could correct this fatal mista—

"*Stop,*" snapped Mrs. Kane. "Pencils down, eyes up." Ari quickly looked down to see how many ovals she had managed to move. Some, but probably not enough to get her promoted to the sixth grade, or wherever this test determined you would go. With her stomach in tight little knots, she surrendered her paper to the front of the room, sat back down, and chewed on her braid.

Mrs. Atwood finally returned with Clarinda, whose illness turned out to be a bad case of butter-flies-in-the-stomach. Mrs. Atwood sent the class out in small bunches to the water fountain. When Ari spotted Danny, she asked, "What did you think of the test?"

"A cinch," he said, bending down for a drink.

"A cinch? Are you kidding me?"

Danny lifted his head, his chin dripping with water. He wiped his sleeve across the bottom half of his face. "Sure. You don't really take those tests seriously, do you?" He looked at Ari, whose face showed him that she did. "Those tests help the school figure out what subjects they should be teaching better. My sister told me. They aren't really testing *you*, Ari."

Martina Wallhoffer nudged Danny out of the way and took over the water fountain. "A lot you know," she said. "These are Official tests that go into your Permanent Record. Every teacher you'll have for the rest of your Life will know what you got. Even the Police get a copy that goes into your file." Ari felt doomed.

"The *police*?" yelled Danny. "The police don't keep files on schoolkids. Well, maybe they do on you, Wallhopper!" Martina squeezed her eyes, nose, and mouth into as ugly a face as she could manage, shook it at Danny, then turned away into the gurgling water.

As Ari started quietly back to the classroom, Danny ran up to her and slapped her lightly on the shoulder. "Hey, it doesn't tell them anything about you at all."

"Only that I don't know what a trapezoid is. I didn't know it was a *shape;* I thought it was that thing acrobats swing on in the circus."

"Don't shweat it, shweethaht," he whispered. "Guess what. Promise not to tell? I did half the test and got bored. Then I filled in the rest of the ovals so that it would spell out my name!"

"Really?"

Danny started running backward toward his classroom, nodding. He looked as though he was about to trip, but he didn't.

"Uh-huh! No problem!" he sang out, just before bumping into Hannah Swensen and a kid from his class. All three fumbled and fell to the floor. "Whoops!" said Danny, untangling himself from the other kids. For a moment Ari wanted to go over to Hannah and ask if she was all right, but Hannah seemed so . . . so by herself that Ari just didn't know what to say to her. They certainly couldn't talk about the test. No doubt Hannah had whizzed through the whole thing, filling in every oval perfectly. Ari watched Hannah smile shyly at Danny, whisk her hair behind her ear, and walk back to the classroom alone.

Mrs. Atwood was at her desk, looking a little wrung out, her hands cupping a fresh mug of coffee.

"People," she announced, "for the remainder of this afternoon, we'll be having remedial relaxation. I think we need it." Everyone knew that this meant indoor recess and cheered wildly. Quickly 5A pulled off their shoes and threw them inside their desks, the first step in remedial relaxation. All talk of the test was then pushed away with the rearranging of desks.

Outside the large windows, it was snowing

lightly. The happy activity inside the classroom made Ari feel like part of a cozy scene inside a little domed paperweight with swirling snow all around. Some kids shoved their desks together and played paper football; others played Hangman with colored chalk on the chalkboard, or Temple of Doom. Hannah sat cutting a paper chain of animals. But a large portion of 5A stood in line, waiting to challenge Mrs. Atwood to a game of Chinese checkers. It was set out on a special board that pulled out of her desk. Whenever someone made lots of mistakes on their homework or test, they would have to sit at Mrs. Atwood's desk with the little board pulled out and watch their paper become a graffiti of red pencil marks. But this afternoon was different. Mrs. Atwood kept her shoes on and her eyebrows arched. She was the Chinese Checkers Champ, and her nostrils flared out a bit as she prepared for her next challenger.

"Okay, Ari, show me what you've got." Ari picked up a marble, then looked at Mrs. Atwood.

"That test we just took," said Ari. "Does it count a *little*-a-lot or a *lot*-a-lot?" Mrs. Atwood's coral lips began their upward slide toward her right ear. Ari felt her face heat up. Please don't make fun of me, she prayed.

"Don't lose any sleep over it, Ari. We just like to throw a good scare into you now and then." Mrs.

Atwood's owl eyes softened with a look that Ari felt could knock her over. Mrs. Atwood's powers were enveloping Ari in her magic aura. If only she could learn to affect people the way Mrs. Atwood did. Forget fractions, definitions, and dangling participles: Ari needed to learn how to be enchanting, scary, wise, and mysterious. Did Mrs. Atwood know that Ari Spire was ready to learn the secret of her powers?

"Your move, Ari," Mrs. Atwood said softy.

How long had Ari been sitting there, staring at her teacher? Ari felt as though she had been hypnotized. To shake herself out of it, she widened her eyes, saying, "Okay, here we go!" and placed her marble on the board. Mrs. Atwood kept her eyes fixed on the checkerboard as she reached for her mug of coffee, took a long sip, then confidently put her marble down. In that moment Ari felt happy and warm all over, even without coffee to sip.

Chapter

"So, where's the magic-potion kit?" Ari twisted through the labyrinth of cartons that filled the front hallway. It was Danny's last day in his house. The bookshelves were empty and the furniture was pushed away from the walls, allowing old dustballs to roll out across the floor. The rooms that had always felt as comfortable and inviting as an unmade bed now felt cold and impersonal.

Danny's mother was efficiently swaddling glasses in newspaper blankets and tucking them into boxes marked FRAGILE. Ari made her way to Danny, who was sitting on a stack of cartons eating an apple and looking grumpy. Danny's mother stopped wrapping and tucked a piece of her frosted blond hair behind her ear. She cocked her head meaningfully toward Danny. Ari understood: She needed Ari's help.

"Ari," said Danny's mother cheerfully, "I've got a roll of chocolate chip cookie dough in the fridge. How 'bout I slice up some raw cookie-dough cubes, and you two can grab some toothpicks and . . ." She pursed her lips and pantomimed eating a small tidbit off a toothpick with extreme delicacy. She looked over at Danny and laughed. "Remember when you and Ari served that as an hors d'oeuvre at our Chanukah party?" Danny rolled his eyes in embarrassment and jumped down from the stack of cartons. Mrs. Ryder smiled at Ari, and Ari felt a clamping in her throat. She missed them already.

"C'mon," said Danny. "I'll show you what came in the mail."

They ran up to his room and slammed the door. Danny disappeared halfway under his bed, then backed out with a box in his hands. Ari carefully took the box and placed it on the bed. She slid out a smaller box labeled SINBAD'S GENUINE MAGIC POTION KIT. As Ari lifted the cover, her eyes grew wide at the assortment of thimble-sized bottles.

"Wow!" she whispered, and gently stroked the tops of the bottles. Then she picked up the outside box to examine the return address.

51

"New *Jersey*?" she said. "I thought the ad said these potions come from the exotic Far East."

Danny shrugged. "Maybe if you live in Omaha, New Jersey *is* the exotic Far East."

"Hmm." Ari removed the ten tiny bottles and placed them on Danny's night table. Together they read aloud the labels and held the bottles up to the lamp to see their different colors. "Tranquillity" was blue, "Prosperity" was purple, "Passion" was red. Then they sniffed a yellow bottle marked BEWITCHINGLY BEAUTIFUL.

"Smells like pee," Danny grunted, and turned away. Ari sniffed it again.

"Does not," she said, turning the bottle to read the label. "See? It says, 'Fruit extracts and all-natural ingredients.'" Danny played with the blinds as Ari rubbed her finger lightly around the rim of the bottle. Then she dabbed it behind one ear.

"Wanna do the Ouija board?" she asked.

Danny shrugged again. "If you want," he said, and they sat cross-legged on the floor, facing each other, the Ouija board balanced between their two laps. Ari set the indicator on the board.

Ari cleared her throat and asked the first question. "Is anything exciting going to happen?" They laid their hands on either side of the indicator and watched the little window with the needle in it as it began to slowly move over the alphabet. *D* was the first letter. Then it slid all the way down to the number 2. Danny looked nervously up at Ari.

"You're not moving it, are you?" she asked. One of them always asked this.

"Nope," he answered, keeping his eyes on the board. The indicator slid back up to the letter *G*, then moved steadily over to *O*.

The indicator moved around, its little needle hovering randomly over letters and numbers, until Ari said, "I think that's all. *D 2 G O*. That must be the message."

Danny looked away from the board, biting the corner of his thumbnail. They were both quiet for a while, and then Ari shot up, sending the board tumbling into Danny's lap.

"You did too move the board!" she yelled. She stood with her arms folded and her lips drawn in tight. "*D*—that stands for Danny, right? Danny to *go*!" Danny stood up and walked over to his dresser. He opened the top drawer and began to sort through his stuff.

"I didn't move it," he said quietly. "And the board didn't lie. 'Danny to Go.' Sounds like a takeout order, huh? A hamburger and Danny to go. Go to a new house. Go to a new stepdad. Go to a new school . . ."

Ari let her arms fall to her sides, and her voice softened. "I know," she said. "It stinks. But at least Frank is nice. He really likes you, and your mom likes him, and you still have your dad, and your dad likes you. . . ." Ari was hoping he'd smile by then, but he didn't.

Instead, he carefully wound his yo-yo as if it were the most important thing in the world.

"I know," he said. "To you, it sounds easy. Just wrap Danny in newspaper and stuff him into a box with the rest of the junk."

Ari studied him like a subtraction problem with way too many zeros. "I didn't say it sounded easy." They both grew quiet. It was the longest time they had ever been silent together, and the first time Ari just wanted to take off, get away from Danny and his cartons and his new life. She fiddled with a bottle, trying to think of something to say. "Well . . . well, just think about the photo in *The Guinness Book of World Records* showing our gum-wrapper chain reaching from Arlington to Winchester . . . it'll be amazing!"

"Yeah, right." Now Danny was examining the dust on his dresser through his magnifying glass.

"You're not going to stop making the chain . . . are you?" said Ari.

Danny slammed the top drawer shut, plopped

down on his bed, and hugged his knees to his chest. "Who cares about *The Guinness Book of World Records*, anyway?"

"You mean you're just gonna drop it, like that? After all our work?"

"Well, what else can we do with it? We'd be eleventy-jillion years old before it reached Winchester. You'll be wearing mail-order teeth by then." He threw his Nerf football at Ari.

"And you'll be wearing diapers for grown-ups!" Ari threw the ball back at him and felt a little better. At least, she thought, we sound like ourselves again. "Still," she said, eyeing the word *good-bye* at the bottom of the Ouija board, "I think we should try and keep it up. Otherwise—it just feels—like—a waste." She looked at Danny anxiously. He was pretending to organize some comic books on his bed.

"Yeah, okay, I guess," he answered.

"I mean, it's not like we can't still visit each other. Lydia took a dance class in Winchester once. It's just a couple of towns over, y'know."

"Yeah," said Danny, "I know." Then he glanced up from his comic book and looked at the boxes from New Jersey. "You can keep those potions—if you want."

"Thanks," said Ari. When they came out on the

front steps, she picked up one of the bottles and held it close. "I think I'll put a drop of Passion into Lydia's soda tonight and see if she falls in love with something besides a walrus."

"I wouldn't bet on it," said Danny, smiling.

Chapter

7

After Danny moved, Ari walked home by herself
every day. It felt strange having the empty air
next to her as she walked, and one time she even
went right past her own house to Danny's. She'd
been thinking about playing Quest for Survival, and
when she arrived at his house and saw the SOLD sign
stuck in the brown grass, she felt sad and stupid. It
was weird, she thought, how you could actually feel
someone's not being there. She imagined it was
even worse for Danny.

As she plodded home day after day, Ari began to
play Quest for Survival in her head. It helped to
keep her mind off the empty air, and besides, it was
important to keep their game going while they were
apart. She imagined Danny played the game in his

head too. Ari decided that Danny had been captured by the Cyclops and trapped in his cave. He was still alive, though, for the Cyclops was fattening him up. It made sense. If Danny were to be eaten right away, he'd be nothing but a scrawny little sparerib: two, three bites at the most, and you'd be sucking on bone. That would never satisfy the tremendous appetite of a Cyclops. So for days Danny had been feasting on roasted leg of lamb (of course, the Cyclops ate its sheep raw) and was quickly becoming a succulent little morsel. Ari spent every day after school sharpening the tip of a long branch, and was finally ready to carry out her rescue plan.

She brought a piece of bread and cheese into the backyard along with her spear, and imagined herself alone in the world. The yard felt appropriately bleak with its stark gray trees and the few stubborn oak leaves clinging to their branches like withered paper bags. As Ari squinted in the cold air, she took a tiny nibble of her food and put it aside. Then she took a few deep breaths and stared purposefully at the tall hedge on the far side of her yard. The Cyclops, having snacked on a few sheep, was taking its afternoon nap. "Now is the best time to do it. I'll sneak into the cave and gouge its eye out while it's still asleep," Ari whispered to herself. Bending forward like a hunter, she moved on tiptoe with quiet, slow steps toward the hedge, careful not to land on twigs that might wake the beast. A high voice behind her made her jump.

"Yaghs!" cried Ari. The spear leapt out of her hand, and she whipped around to find Erica Finn staring at her.

"Whatcha doing?" asked Erica. Erica was a second-grader who lived a few houses down from Ari.

Ari sighed loudly and sauntered over to Erica. "You shouldn't sneak up on people, Erica. It's rude."

"Are you playing something?"

"Not anymore," said Ari. She never wanted to play with Erica because she was bossy and whiny and always mad at someone.

"Oh, pleeease?" said Erica. "Can't I play with you for just a little? Pleeease?" Ari bit the inside of one cheek as she sized up Erica. True, Erica was a real Miss Bossy Pants, but playing Quest for Survival alone wasn't that much fun, and besides, Erica might be good for fetching things or digging holes.

"Well . . ." Ari snapped the spit in her mouth. "Okay. For a little bit."

"What're we playing?" asked Erica, her eyes widening. Ari squatted on the grass, and Erica immediately dropped down too.

"Well, over in that bush, there's this cave, and in that cave is a one-eyed monster called a Cyclops.

And Dann—I mean this boy—is trapped in there, and we have to get him out before the Cyclops wakes up and eats him for supper."

Erica nodded solemnly at Ari.

"But first you have to take half of my cheese and bread. This is the only food you'll have for days, so you better make it last." Ari folded the cheese in half, then tore the bread in half, and handed them to Erica. "Now, here's what we have to do," she whispered. "I'm going to sneak into the cave and blind the Cyclops with my spear. This way, Da—the boy—can escape. Then we're going to capture him in a deep hole. You start digging the hole over there, and I'll lead the Cyclops into the trap with my voice. You can use that small shovel by the fence."

Erica's brow furrowed. "That's not fair," she whined. "All I get to do is dig a stupid hole while you have all the fun. Let's make it so the Cyclops eats the boy and then tries to get us, too!"

Ari stared at her, shocked. "He can't eat the boy! I have to rescue him! He's my friend. I'm not just gonna let him get eaten!"

"But then it's no fun for *me*. I wanna play it my way."

"Look, do you want to play with me or not?"

Erica's mouth puckered. "Oh, okay," she grumbled. She stood up and tramped off, her arms swinging angrily as she headed for the step where the shovel was lying. She grabbed the shovel and squatted down, pouting as she stabbed the cold ground.

Ari picked up her spear and resumed her stealthy advance toward the bush. She made her way slowly to make it seem longer, then looked around and pulled her arm back, aiming up at the Cyclops's eye. Just as she was about to let the spear fly, Erica came running up behind her and shrieked. Ari dropped the spear, point down, on her own foot.

"Yowch!" cried Ari.

"Eeeeekk! The Cyclops is awake! The Cyclops is awake!" screeched Erica. "It's after us! Run, Ari!" Erica ran in circles all over the yard, her cheese flapping in one hand, the bread in the other. From time to time she glanced back with terror at the invisible Cyclops chasing her. Ari stood still, her hands on her hips, and said nothing until Erica was crouched in a far corner of the yard, panting. Ari took her time walking over to Erica and glowered at her.

"You were supposed to be digging a hole," Ari said stonily.

"I didn't want to."

"Well, I don't play with babies who don't listen."

"And I don't play with bossy people," said Erica, stuffing all the cheese into her mouth.

"Takes one to know one," snapped Ari. "You don't

understand how this game works, Erica. You can't just do whatever you want to do. There's a *plan*, and both people agree to the plan, get it? But of course you don't." Ari's voice was steadily rising, and now Erica was looking more afraid of Ari than she was of any Cyclops. "You're just a whiny little bossy-butt who doesn't listen, and if you *can't* listen and understand how it works, you *can't* play!"

Erica's eyes filled with tears. The bread was squished in her hand like Silly Putty. She tossed it on the ground.

"You're mean, Ari!" she cried. She lifted her dirt-streaked face up at Ari, stuck out her tongue, then ran out of the yard.

Ari stood for a while in the cold, grinding the tip of her sneaker hard into the ground. She had never thought of herself as mean, but Erica hadn't listened, and she had totally ruined the game. With Danny it always flowed so easily. It just worked. It was *their* game. But without Danny it didn't work. Ari abandoned her spear and trudged back inside.

"Mom, where's that piece of paper with Danny's new phone number?" Ari leaned against the kitchen door frame. Her mother was busy constructing a lasagna, smearing a layer of ricotta across a huge pan. She put down the spatula, and as she turned to get the paper from a drawer, she stopped and stared at Ari.

"What?" said Ari defensively. Why did mothers always have to stare?

"I think we need to go shopping soon," said her mother.

"Why?"

"Look down, Ari."

Ari looked down and saw that her favorite purple jeans had shrunk. "Mom! Did you wash these in hot water?"

"Noooo. You've grown, my little chickadee!" Ari's mother smiled slyly, and Ari turned away, embarrassed. "It's nothing to be ashamed of, Ari. You're growing and your clothes just don't fit anymore. Most girls would be happy to hear that they need new clothes. I think before we hit the stores, though, I'll make a trip to the attic and see what we have in the way of Lydia hand-me-downs."

Ari tugged on her pants and sullenly took the paper with the phone number from her mother.

"Hello, Mrs. Ryder? Hi, it's Ari. Fine, how're you? . . . We miss you guys, too. . . . Oh, I'm glad you don't have to worry about dinners for a while, either. Yeah, Mom tends to cook that way. Uh-huh. Well, I was wondering, is Danny there? Oh. Gymnastics? Yeah, it sure helps to be involved in sports. That's great that he's made friends so quickly. No, it's nothing important. I'll catch him another time. Sure. Thanks. Okay, bye."

"How's Danny?" Ari heard her mother ask behind her.

"He's fine," Ari answered, stomping up the stairs. Just fine and dandy, she thought, out having pizza with friends from gymnastics. Friends! He's the new kid, for crying out loud. How could he have *friends* already? Ari threw herself on her bed and stared at the ceiling. I can't believe I was actually trying to rescue you. You didn't need me. Ari stared at the long stretch of ankle that displayed itself beyond the hem of her pants. She sprang up from her bed, ran downstairs, and marched back out to the yard.

Retrieving the spear, she went down the street to Danny's house. It was still empty, so she quickly made for the backyard. Standing in the center of the yard, she stopped to look up at the window of Danny's old room. For the first time, the backyard that she had played in through leaves, snow, and sprinklers felt lonely and eerie, like a deserted movie set. Ari tightened her grip on the spear, lifted it back, and hurled it forward with all her might. As soon as it flew from her hand, she twisted away and started to leave. Who cared about a stupid old branch? She couldn't help it; she looked back over her shoulder and there it was: dead center in the brambly hedge that had once been the cave of the horrible Cyclops.

Chapter

8

"Y'know, one good thing about Danny moving," said Lydia, standing in the doorway of Ari's room. She was eating an apple and had to keep wiping the juice that was running down her chin. Ari looked up at her from the niche between her bed and her bookshelf. She threw Lydia her best Martina Wallhoffer stare.

"Is what?" she said, biting off the *t* sound.

"Well, for one thing"—*slurp, slurp*, wipe chin—"it'll push you out of the little playhouse you've been hiding in with Danny and force you to"—*crunch*—"make some new friends."

"I haven't been *hiding* in any *playhouse*, and I don't think I should be *forced* to be friends with *anyone*," Ari replied. She turned back to her magazine.

There it was, that ad that had been around since her mother was a kid: "Be a Model . . . Or Just Look Like One." Ari considered it for a moment. How could you decide to "just look like one" if you were really ugly? It didn't make sense.

"What I mean," continued Lydia, "is that you and Danny have been friends since you were in diapers—"

"*Not* true," Ari interjected.

"—and, well, you're not going to stay a little kid forever . . . and it's like . . . you and Danny are like . . . well, it's like you're stuck."

"Why don't *you* stick it." Ari was definitely getting better at this snappy comeback stuff. "And get your face out of my room."

Lydia was sucking on the apple core. "Fine, hairball. I just think it's time to put away the Tinkertoys and stretch a little, that's all." She disappeared out of the doorway, and Ari felt her face grow hot.

" 'Put away the Tinkertoys,' " she said, crimping her voice. Lydia, you are so incredibly vomitous! she thought. What did Lydia want her to do? Roll over on her back and giggle on the phone with Martina about pimply walruses? Besides, Lydia was a fine one to talk. Two large drops of Passion dropped into Lydia's soda hadn't made her even slightly romantic. Maybe a walrus lover needed a higher dose. For the rest of the week she would add one drop to Lydia's drink at suppertime.

That evening Ari found it impossible to study. Each time she began to read her social studies book, the words on the page went blurry and her mind quickly wandered away from "The Exports of Spain." The only export on her mind was Danny. She put down her book and went to visit her father in his study.

Mr. Spire's study was a small room off the living room. It was dark, disorganized, and warm from the computer's constant humming. For some unknown reason, it always had a vague scent of lemons, and its coziness reminded Ari of the niche in her own room. I guess we're alike that way, she thought. Instead of comic books, tabloids, and gossip magazines, though, Mr. Spire's shelves were filled with books about ancient history and mythology. Ever since she could remember, Ari's father had told his daughters stories from Roman or Greek mythology. While other kids knew all about Snow White or the Three Billy Goats Gruff, Lydia and Ari knew the many ways in which Zeus, the supreme god on Mount Olympus, drove his wife, Hera, crazy with jealousy by falling in love with human women.

Once Ari and her sister had overheard a guest call their father Mr. Myth. Ever since then, whenever their father got the look on his face that signaled an oncoming story, Ari and Lydia would lisp, "Uh-oh, here comth Mithter Myth." Nowadays, Lydia groaned when their father launched into myth mode, but Ari still enjoyed the familiar stories.

Ari peeked in the door. Her father was sitting at his desk awash in papers, wearing his favorite blue-gray sweater.

"Oh, Mithter Myth?" said Ari. She felt better instantly.

"Yeth?" her father answered without looking up.

"What are you doing?" She walked over to him and laid a hand on his long back. The sweater was soft like a baby's blanket.

"Grading papers."

"Gross. Was it a test?"

"Yep." Ari could never believe her father was one of those people who walked up and down the aisles of a classroom solemnly handing out papers with red ink marks. To Ari he was just someone who told stories, picked up the dry cleaning on Saturdays, and made a decent tuna sandwich.

"Getting ready for bed?" he asked, still not looking up.

"I guess," Ari replied, playing with his stapler. She watched her father's hand as he scratched his pen back and forth, back and forth, making pointy peaks like the graphs on doctor shows. Her father always used a fountain pen, which he filled from time to time from the bottle of ink on his desk. Ari hated that little bottle. It looked like a mean grown-up just waiting for you to mess up. Next to the ink bottle was a baby picture of Ari pushing up on her elbows, showing a few wispy hairs and a toothless grin. Ari picked it up. How could she and that toothless dumpling be the same person?

"Daddy, why did you name me Ariadne?" she asked as she began shooting staples into the trash. Staplers were amazing.

He kept on scribbling. "Ask your mother."

"I did. She said to ask you."

Ari's father smiled to himself. "It was our trip to Europe. We didn't even know we were expecting you. But your mother was feeling tired and a little nauseous. When we got back home, she found out she was going to have a baby."

"Me!" chirped Ari.

"And because Europe is named for the goddess Europa, we decided to name you for the goddess's loyal and courageous granddaughter, Ariadne. I think that's why we chose it." Mr. Spire kept reading papers as he spoke.

"Thank you for not naming me Europa," Ari said. "But I want to hear about Ariadne. I like that story."

"You know all about your name," said her father, shuffling through his papers. Ari scrunched her face and began chewing on the end of her braid.

"Please."

"Ari, I'm really busy."

"*Ariadne*," she pleaded.

"Very well," sighed her father. He pulled her toward him. "Well, we all know that Ariadne was the beautiful daughter"—he gently pulled Ari's hair out of her mouth—"of King Minos." Ari's father looked back at his pile of papers.

"More!" Ari said.

"Every nine years," said her father, "the king demanded that seven youths and seven maidens from Athens be sent to his island to be devoured by the Minotaur, his monstrous son, who was half bull and half human. The Minotaur was kept in a large maze so that no one could escape, including the monster. But when Theseus arrived—"

"Oh, Thee-see-us!" Ari sighed, batting her eyes like a lovesick girl.

"Exactly," Ari's father said, smiling. "Ariadne fell in love with him and decided to save his life. So, after he performed his amazing gymnastics—"

"While riding a bull," added Ari.

"Right—she gave him a sword and a weighted ball of string that rolled through the maze, guiding him right to where the Minotaur was sleeping. Sure enough, Theseus killed the Minotaur and sailed back to Athens with the others, taking Ariadne with him—"

"But," Ari interrupted.

"But on their way they stopped on the island of Naxos, where Theseus abandoned Ariadne while she was sleeping."

"The crumb," said Ari. "Then what?"

"Oh, well," said her father, turning toward his papers, "she spent a lot of time crying, watching soap operas, and cursing Theseus."

"*Daddy.*"

Ari's father took her onto his lap. "Happily, the god Dionysus found Ariadne, and they fell in love and married. For her wedding present, he gave her a glorious golden crown full of gems. And when she died, he threw her crown into the sky, where the gems turned into stars." Her father gave her forehead a gentle kiss.

"And you can still see it, 'cause it's one of the constellations!" said Ari, lifting her braid into a circle over her head.

"Righto. It was fixed in the heavens a long, long time ago. And now I think it's time for all aspiring goddesses to ascend back up Mount Slumber."

"Huh?"

"Bedtime. It's late."

"Oh," said Ari. "Righto."

Ari's father looked down at her bunny slippers. "Hmm—don't you think it's time you threw those out and got some new slippers? Those look pretty shot."

"Trash Pyramus and Thisbe?" Ari examined her slippers. They were gray with dirt and so old she couldn't remember not having them. The left-foot slipper, Pyramus, had whiskers missing on one side. Thisbe, the right-foot slipper, had a plastic eye that was barely held on by its flimsy thread. Whenever she walked the eye would flip-flop from side to side.

"Well . . . I guess they are kind of wilted," she admitted, slipping off her father's lap and shuffling out of his study. Then she turned around quickly.

"Maybe I'll take some thumbtacks and mount them on my wall like a trophy. That way I can always look at them."

"Good night, Ariadne," said her father.

"Or I know! I'll hang them from some wire hangers, and I can have a bunny-slipper mobile!"

"Sweet dreams, Ari," said her father firmly.

" 'Night, Daddy," said Ari as she and her bedraggled bunnies shuffled out of the room.

Ari liked being told to go to bed. It felt cozier than just deciding for herself when to turn out the lights, the way her sister did. But tonight when she tried to sleep, Ari felt restless, and the comfort she had felt in her father's study drained away while Lydia's words filled the dark room: ". . . You're not going to stay a little kid forever. . . . It's like you're stuck."

When she finally did fall asleep, Ari dreamed she was in an enormous stone maze. In one of the passages was her reading niche, where she was hiding from the Minotaur. In the distance, she could see Danny performing handstands on the back of a bull and laughing, while she sat frantically counting and re-counting a pile of box tops. She was sure that she had the right number, yet no matter how many times she counted, some faceless voice kept telling her that she'd never have enough to send away for the glorious golden crown studded with micro sparkle points.

"**D**id you see the new family move into Danny's house?" said Lydia.

"Are you ever going to learn how to knock?" Ari peeked out from the latest issue of *Star Daze.* Lydia turned down the cassette player. All day long Ari had been listening to sad musicals. She'd reread three stacks of comic books through *Les Misérables,* and now she was wading through her gossip magazines to the moody strains of *Carousel.*

"They've got little kids," said Lydia. "I'm gonna bring the parents some zucchini bread. Who knows? Maybe they need a baby-sitter." Lydia rubbed her thumb against her fingers in the universal money sign. Ari put her nose back into her magazine.

"Is that why you came in here? To tell me about all the money you're going to make watching TV and eating Fig Newtons? That's swell, Lydia. I'm so happy for you."

"Oh, c'mon, Ari—" Lydia began, but Ari suddenly scrambled out of her niche, turned up the volume, and signaled with her finger against her lips for Lydia to hush. The mushiest song of all, "When You Walk Through a Storm," was beginning, and Ari wasn't going to miss the chance to wallow in it. She crawled back into her niche and, having read all of *Star Daze*, picked up *The Weekly Comet*. "The Shape of Your Pinky Toe Reveals How Long You'll Live!" read the headline. This looked interesting.

"God, Ariadne, what is with you? You're becoming such a weird little snot. Talk about your pyucks! Why don't you get rid of your *Weekly Vomit* and get an actual life? Very soon, you're gonna start to rot in here, and no one'll want to come near you because you'll smell so bad."

"I *vant* to be *alone*," proclaimed Ari from behind her newspaper. Lydia snorted and left.

Ari had seen the new family move in that morning. She had watched the new kids riding their bikes over Danny's lawn and carrying strange furniture through Danny's front door. All morning she had felt a hollowness in her stomach, as though someone had taken a cold metal ice-cream scoop and scooped out her center. Everyone in her family wanted to cheer her up. Her mother offered to take her out for shopping and a sundae, and her father tried to talk her into riding bikes. But Ari didn't want to be cheered up. She just wanted to be sad for a while. That seemed to drive her family nuts.

She thought of the first phone call she had had with Danny from his new house. They had only been apart for a couple of weeks, but on the phone it had felt like years. Ari realized she and Danny had hardly ever spoken on the phone. To make plans, yes; but to chat? Never.

Danny: Ari? Hi, it's Danny, how're you?

Ari: Fine. How are you?

Danny: All right.

Ari: How's your house?

Danny: All right.

Ari: How's your mom and Frank?

Danny: All right.

Ari: Danny, are you sure everything's all right?

Danny: (snort of laughter) Yeah, everything's great. So, um, seen any good movies lately?

Ari: Not really.

Danny: Me neither. Well, maybe I'll see you sometime soon.

Ari: Yeah, that'd be great.

Danny: Okay, bye.
Ari: Bye.

Yilch! Maybe she should try writing him a letter instead.

The thought of mail roused her from her niche, and she went downstairs and stepped out the door to see if anything had come for her. She flipped open the top of the black metal box, pulled out a promising thick pile, and with her index finger flipped quickly through the envelopes. Yes! Her career and personality survey from the back of *The Weekly Comet* had arrived, and, cheered by the sight of her name on the envelope, she ran to her room and ripped it open.

Dear Miss Spire,

It takes luck and talent to succeed. Fortunately, you have both! Your responses to our survey demonstrate creativity, an independent nature as well as a keen aptitude for problem solving.

Ari flipped over the paper.

The Institute for Success has determined that you have a promising career in refrigerator re-

pair, and sincerely hopes that you will make a positive change in your life. . . .

Ari gulped. Refrigerator repair? Then she read on and discovered that they wanted her to fork over *one hundred dollars and ninety-five cents* in order to *Get Started Today on the Road to Success and Personal Achievement.* Talk about your mega–rip-offs! Ari crumpled up the letter and threw it across her room.

Then she took out her gum-wrapper chain and inhaled its sugary smell. But instead of feeling better, she got a lump in her stomach. She stuffed the chain back into its box.

Downstairs, Ari sat at the kitchen table dunking cookies into milk. A full-page ad caught her eye.

"Cassandra's Psychic Oracles—Reveal Your Future." Ari began nibbling the end of her braid. This looked good. Really good.

Long before modern science, ancient civilizations understood many secrets of the universe. Now you can uncover the mystery of your past and future through the psychic powers of Cassandra's Oracles. Discover the ancient wisdom of the oracle. Let Cassandra's predictions reveal your true destiny!

78

"My true destiny," Ari said aloud. Maybe this one was for real. After all, her father had told her how the ancient Egyptians and ancient Greeks understood astronomy thousands of years before computers and high-powered telescopes. Perhaps this Cassandra knew these ancient secrets because she was descended from the priests of the Delphic oracle. And didn't the ancient Greeks consult the Delphic oracle to learn their "true destiny"? Ari's heart was beginning to pound. After all, she was an Ariadne, and surely Cassandra would recognize her as a kind of ancient soul mate. Cassandra could reveal all the extraordinary things that would happen and tell her what to do now that Danny was gone. Ari's eyes traveled down the page. *$3.99 per minute. Must be 18 years or older. 24-hour service.* Four dollars for one minute? Ari's hair was soggy by now, and she was twirling the very tips into a sharp point. Well, how long could it take to reveal one's true destiny? Couldn't be more than three minutes. Of course there was the age thing, but Ari could disguise her voice. Make it a little lower and more serious. Like Lydia's. Her parents were out, so Ari went to the phone and dialed.

"This call will be charged to this phone number," said a clipped, nasal voice. Then the voice recited Ari's phone number. For an exotic psychic, the voice on the phone sure sounded a lot like a telephone operator's.

"Yes," Ari answered in her deep movie-star voice, "that's my phone number."

The nasal voice told her to hold a moment for Cassandra. Ari heard a beep like an answering machine, and then a voice even more movie-starish than Ari's congratulated her on choosing Cassandra to reveal the mystery of the future. "Cassandra is the one oracle you can believe," continued the breathy voice, and Ari started watching the digits on the clock change. Was Cassandra going to take up the whole three minutes with a commercial for herself? "Do you have any questions for me about your future?"

"Well," Ari began, remembering to keep her voice low and steady, "I'd like to know a little bit about my true destiny."

"Is there someone special in your life?" asked Cassandra.

"Yes," answered Ari. "But he just moved away."

"I see," said Cassandra. "I sense that you're still attached to this person and that you're feeling a little lost without him."

"Yes." Wow, this Cassandra lady was amazing.

"And when he moved, did he leave a token of himself with you?" Ari thought of the magic-potion bottles.

"Yes."

"Then I feel that this person also has a strong attachment to you, that there is something connecting the two of you." The gum-wrapper chain! Ari began to feel both frightened and excited by Cassandra's powers.

"Yes, there is!" Ari said. "How did you know that?"

"Do many people know of this connection between the two of you?" asked Cassandra.

"Only a few," said Ari. "Most people wouldn't understand; they'd take it the wrong way."

"Of course. And that special connection you have will bring him back to you."

"Really?"

"Yes, but you must be patient. And you must take care of yourself—for your sake and for the baby's."

"Baby!" screamed Ari, totally forgetting her phony voice. Cassandra gave a muffled chuckle, then composed herself.

"You also need to know that I sense someone else who wants to get closer to you."

Ari's head swam with faces, but mostly she saw Martina's. Martina? What kind of a destiny was that? And where'd Cassandra get this stuff about a baby? She was way off the mark on that one.

"I must tell you that in the money sphere, you will experience some hardship before things get better, but they will indeed get better. I can guide you toward ways to quickly improve your situation, but we'll need to talk longer. Would you like me to tell you what I see as your path to financial success?"

"Okay—I mean *no!*" Ari looked at the clock. Her three minutes were definitely up.

"Very well, then. Thank you for consulting me and tapping into my powers of prediction. I look forward to revealing more of your exciting future to you." The phone beeped, and Ari stood frozen for a moment with it in her hand. Did I really just do that? she thought, and hung up the phone. Wow. An encounter with the oracle.

When she was back in her room, Ari examined her pinky toe on her right foot. As far as she could tell, its shape resembled a backward letter *C*, which according to the article belonged to people who were "passionate and stubborn." This was bad for one's health and meant Ari could expect to kick the bucket at sixty-two. Until then, it would be a life of financial hardship, broken refrigerators, and Martina Wallhoffer. But no babies. Definitely no babies.

Chapter

10

The next morning Ari entered her classroom and her heart sank. A substitute. And not just any substitute, but Mrs. Zwort, the meanest substitute of all the subs who circulated in the school. Even worse, she told the class that Mrs. Atwood would be out for days. *Days.* Ari couldn't believe Mrs. Atwood would abandon her like this. Without Danny around, she needed more than ever to watch Mrs. Atwood's face, to see her run her fingers through the left side of her hair and make kids squirm.

Ari chewed on the end of her braid and stared dismally at the sub. Mrs. Zwort wore a too-tight lime-green suit that was made from some nubby material that would surely prick you like a cactus if you got too close. The only part of substituting she seemed to enjoy was standing at the blackboard and writing down the names of kids who misbehaved. In her harsh, raspy voice, she would spell out the names as she wrote them, like a warped version of Hangman. "Martindale," she'd boom, *"M-A-R-T-I-N-D-A-L-E."* That done, she'd brush the chalk dust off the tips of her fingers and suck in her cheeks as she walked briskly back to the desk. If anyone continued to misbehave, or just ticked her off, they would get a check next to their name. Peter already had two checks and it wasn't even lunch. At least, thought Ari, her own name wasn't up there.

Mrs. Zwort nervously sifted through some papers on Mrs. Atwood's desk. "I'm going to announce the winners of the Dental Hygiene Contest," she said sourly, as if the idea of having any winners in this class was truly distasteful. The class grew quiet and expectant.

"First prize goes to Hannah Swensen."

Figures, thought Ari. She'd get first prize in a toilet-flushing contest. Hannah was not only the fifth-grade brain but also had great handwriting and graciously put up with everyone calling her Ha-nah Ba-na-nah. Hannah hesitated in getting up from her seat, uncertain how this ceremony was to be conducted.

When Hannah came to the front of the room,

Mrs. Zwort handed her a blue ribbon, along with a small pink plastic cup that had a see-through cover. Inside were a tiny toothbrush, toothpaste, and dental floss. It looked like a pencil kit for a child dentist.

"This is Hannah's winning poster." Mrs. Zwort held up the large piece of poster board. Ari's mouth fell open. The Scarecrow, Lion, and Tin Man were cleaning their teeth! A small citizen of Oz, all dressed in green, held a scroll that read:

> *Brush, brush here,*
> *Floss, floss there,*
> *The reason is because,*
> *That's how you keep a healthy mouth,*
> *In the merry old land of Oz!*

All eyes followed Hannah enviously as she made her way back to her seat. She nervously tucked a piece of her stringy yellow hair behind her ear and quietly handed around her prize to the kids who sat by her. Ari stared with wonder at Hannah.

"Second prize goes to Brian Tucker."

"Yes!" Brian shouted, punching the air with a victorious fist. He ran up to the teacher's desk and claimed his red ribbon, along with a page of goofy smiling-teeth stickers. Ari couldn't believe it. Mr. Happy Tooth was grinning his big toothy grin while Miss Toothbrush smiled with outstretched arms.

Brushing Is Fun and Gets the Job Done! read Brian's poster.

Ari was busy studying his artwork when she heard Mrs. Zwort say, "And honorable mention goes to Ari Spire." Martina Wallhoffer threw her a look that Ari couldn't read—was she mad at her for winning? Or just surprised? Mrs. Zwort handed Ari a yellow ribbon and a booklet about caring for your teeth. Then Mrs. Zwort studied Ari's poster and furrowed her brow. "Well, this certainly is unusual," she said, turning the poster around to the class.

"Wow, that's good," murmured some of the kids up front, admiring the graveyard of little tooth tombstones. On each tooth was an epitaph written in tiny writing. One such tooth read: *In a Rush and Didn't Brush. R.I.P.* Another said: *Dull and Yellow, a Rotten Fellow*. Mrs. Zwort eyed Ari suspiciously. "All right, Miss Spire, you may take your seat." Mrs. Zwort never called the students by their first names. Feeling her face flush, Ari rushed back to her seat, eager for the moment to be over.

"Well," said Mrs. Zwort, reading her notes, "it says here to congratulate you all for your original and creative work." Her quick, cold glance at the class let them know that this was all the congratulations they were going to get from her. She looked back at her notes. "The winning posters will be displayed downstairs and the rest will be returned at the end of the day. Hmm. You have the next five minutes to write in your journals." Floppy blue notebooks fluttered from the desks.

Ari liked having a school journal because it gave her a chance to speak in private with Mrs. Atwood. No one else at school knew how much she missed Danny, and she liked the fact that her teacher knew most of the old movies she mentioned. Ari opened her notebook, but she felt as though her brain and hand were disconnected. There was nothing she wanted to share with this sub, so she just reported the weather and what she ate for lunch.

"You should've won first prize," said Martina later, as she ran her fingers over Ari's ribbon. "I thought your poster was the best. Don't you think you should've won?"

"I don't know." Ari shrugged. The class was putting away their journals and getting ready for math. Martina leaned in close to Ari. Martina always smelled fresh and herbal.

"I thought Hannah's was stupid," she whispered, then laughed. She waited for Ari's reaction.

"I don't know," Ari said nervously. She wasn't sure what Martina wanted from her. She glanced over at Hannah, sharpening her pencil at her desk and chatting with her neighbor. "Her poster was okay. She's a good artist."

"She's a goody-goody, you mean."

"No, I—I don't mean that," replied Ari. "I mean, she's sort of a goody-goody, but—" Under Martina's watchful eye, Ari didn't know how she really felt about anything. She felt like the Scarecrow, Tin Man, and Lion all wrapped up in one: no brains, no heart, no guts. Ari avoided Martina's eye as anger and fear welled up inside her. "Actually, Hannah's kind of—nice. She's just—y'know—good at a lot of things." Martina cocked her head to consider this, and Ari knew that she had given the wrong answer.

They were suddenly interrupted by Mrs. Zwort handing out a surprise math test.

"This test is on reciprocal fractions," droned Mrs. Zwort. "You have exactly twenty minutes, and the only sound I want to hear is silence."

The class quickly became a roomful of grunts, heavy breathing, and squeaking seats. Ari was aware that Martina's eyes were on her. She looked up and saw Martina trying to catch her attention. Martina pointed with her pencil to problem number four. At first Ari was confused, but Martina's repeated stabbing of her eraser on number four made it clear what she wanted. Ari didn't know what to do. She looked away, and for a moment her eyes were fixed on Hannah. Then Ari put her chin in her hand and, shielding her mouth, silently formed the word *sixty-three*. With her hand hanging down just below her seat, she flashed the fractional remainder with her fingers. Martina nodded and starting writing.

"Eyes on your own papers," said Mrs. Zwort. Without looking up, Ari knew that the voice was aimed in her direction. A few moments passed, and she felt Martina's eyes tugging at her once again. Martina was stuck on number fifteen. Ari mouthed the answer. She felt her paper being pulled out from under her hands and looked up into the sour face of Mrs. Zwort.

"You'll wait in the hall until you're told to come in." Ari got up from her seat and felt the whole class at her back as she left the room. She had meant to catch Martina's eyes to see what she would do, but her body could barely handle the struggle of lifting itself out of its chair and moving through the buzzing room. The door behind her shut with a loud *click.*

Once outside her classroom, Ari tried sorting out the jumble of emotions pounding through her body. Anger and shame whirled like a hurricane inside her head, and her heart was whining in humiliation. It's not fair! How can this be happening to me? she thought. The Zwort had declared, *"Off with her head!"* without even asking if she was guilty or innocent.

"Atwood, how could you do this to me? How could you sacrifice *me* to that—that dragon lady?

89

You know I need you to be here now!" Ari chewed angrily on her braid, thinking about how everyone in her world was just abandoning her and how incredibly unfair it all was.

The hallway was empty and quiet, and, already bored beyond belief, Ari spread her arms out and flattened her body against the cool stone wall. She pretended she was Olivia de Havilland in the old movie *The Snake Pit*. Ari loved it because it took place in the worst imaginable mental institution. Ari opened her eyes as wide as they would go and looked from side to side, imagining that she was surrounded by clawing crazy people. Now came the part when Olivia went berserk. Ari cupped her hand around her eyes and pantomimed a long, agonizing scream. Just as she was reaching her dramatic climax, she heard the rumble of a class downstairs, on its way back to the second floor. Her heart sped up, and she dropped her hands. To be banished from the class was bad enough, but to be displayed out here like the first-prize winner of the Rotten Kid Contest was too much.

The rumble got louder, and even more dreadful was the realization that the noisy class on the stairs was being led by her third-grade teacher, Ms. Loomis. Ms. Loomis was young and always wore huge, flashy earrings.

And now there she was, a small, pretty voice in the stairwell that soon would materialize into a shocked, disappointed grown-up. She would probably stop her class and say, "Why, Ari Spire, what are you doing in the hallway? You used to be such a good kid. I guess you didn't turn out so well after all." It was a fate worse than death. Ari wouldn't allow it.

She looked around at the gray-green walls and up at the fluorescent lights, and then at the chair right outside the next classroom. She pulled the chair over and stood on it, facing the wall where pictures and stories hung from a strip of cork that ran the full length of the hallway. Working quickly, she removed most of the papers pinned on either side of her class door. She put the papers in a neat pile on the floor and kept the thumbtacks in her hand. Then she began picking up the papers and pinning them back onto the cork.

As Ms. Loomis's class approached, Ari felt herself begin to shake, not certain that she could pull this off. She turned around as soon as she caught a whiff of the teacher's perfume.

"Oh, hi, Ms. Loomis!" she called, a little too loudly.

Ms. Loomis didn't stop walking but slowed down as she said, "Hi, Ari. Looks like you're doing a good job." She smiled her enchanting smile at Ari. As the third-graders moved past her, Ari felt like Dorothy looking down at all the little munchkins. The third-graders looked up admiringly at the student who was so outstanding that she had been chosen over all her classmates to perform this privileged task.

Once the class turned the corner, Ari worked furiously to get the rest of the papers up before anyone came out of her own classroom.

Just as she was pressing in the last thumbtacks, one of the Dingles popped her head out the door and looked up at Ari.

"You can come in now." Ari gave a startled gasp and looked at her as if she were a ghost. Then the door shut and the Dingle was gone. The chair started to slide out from under Ari with a screech that echoed in the hallway, and her knee banged hard against the chair. It hurt a lot, and Ari wanted to grab hold of it. Instead, she tried to ignore the throbbing and strode proudly back into the classroom.

As she took her seat, Ari felt her whole body sag at the sight of her name misspelled on the board. Oh, swell, she thought, now I'm Ara*idne*. She silently checked in with Martina, who looked at her with her tightly buttoned lips and wide-open eyes that said, "Oh my, poor you." The book monitor came by and slapped a *Weekly Reader* down on her desk for Sustained Reading Time. Ari adjusted her glasses and brought the *Weekly Reader* up close for a quick whiff of its sweet, woody newsprint. She was thrilled to be back in her own seat.

Martina avoided her until they were getting ready to go home. Then she whispered, "I'm really sorry you got kicked out during the test."

"If you're so sorry, how come you didn't say anything?" Ari kept her face down, busily stuffing her books into her backpack.

"It all happened so quickly, I didn't even know you had been caught."

Ari looked up, and through her teeth whispered loudly, "*I'd* been caught? *You* got me into this mess."

"I know . . . and you're a really great friend for helping me. I'll help you with any homework or project that comes up. I swear. Is she going to let you take a makeup?"

"Why should she? She thinks it was *me* who was cheating. Plus I get the honor of having my name— ha-ha—on the board." Ari looked up at Martina's freckled nose. "Unless I say something." She watched with satisfaction as a glimmer of panic flashed on Martina's pretty face. Then Ari turned her attention to the impossible zipper on her coat.

"Y'know, you're really lucky, Ari. I mean, you're smart and teachers like you. I don't think Mrs. Atwood likes me."

"She likes you," Ari said uneasily. "She always says how nice you look."

"Yeah, but I can tell. You know how she looks at people like she's got X-ray vision or something. And she's called my parents about my schoolwork." Ari looked up and saw Martina nervously chewing on her lip. "If I didn't get a good grade on this math test, my parents'd kill me. You're such a good friend to help me." Ari didn't say anything. She heaved her backpack onto her shoulders and started out of the cloakroom.

"Wait, Ari!" said Martina brightly. Ari stopped and turned. "Come to my house today! Oh, wait, my mother's working late. Let's go to yours!"

Ari felt a slight buzzing in her head. "My house?" she asked weakly. This was happening too fast. Cassandra had predicted this would happen. "I don't know. I think my mom's taking me shopping for shoes today."

"You just got shoes!" said Martina.

Drats! thought Ari. How could I be so stupid?

"Just for a little while," Martina pleaded. She tilted her head and said, "I'm sorry. Really. C'mon, it'll be fun." Martina dug into her tote bag and wrapped something in her fist. She held it out to

Ari. "Here, I want you to have this." She opened her fist and presented Ari with a key chain attached to a tiny Magic Eight Ball.

Ari's mouth watered. She loved Magic Eight Balls, but she shifted into automatic polite. "You don't have to," she said.

"No, really," pleaded Martina. "I don't want it. My cousin gave it to me. It's not really my kind of thing."

"Well, are you sure?"

"Uh-huh."

"Okay. . . . Thanks," and Ari took it from Martina's sweaty palm.

"So, can I come to your house, pleeease?" Ari turned the tiny Eight Ball over and peered through its tiny window for the answer.

" 'My Sources Say Yes,' " she quoted.

Chapter

11

Martina walked slowly around Ari's room as if she were sifting through stuff at a junk sale. She picked up Ari's things and examined them, making little "hmphing" sounds as she turned them around in her hands. Ari sat on her bed watching Martina, waiting to see which of her things would earn the Martina Seal of Approval. Nothing did. Martina turned to her. "Do you have a diary?"

"No. I mean, I used to. But it was more like a spy journal."

"You spy on people?" Martina asked hopefully.

"Well, I used to. I tried. But it didn't work. I always got caught."

"Oh," said Martina. Ari looked around her room

for something that might interest Martina. She went to her bookshelf.

"Do you like comics?" asked Ari, and Martina smiled, crouching down next to Ari where the comics were piled.

"Sure," said Martina. "Do you have any love comics?"

"I don't think so," Ari answered, knowing full well that her mother forbade them. "But I have lots of others. Actually, what I really like are the ads at the back of these magazines." Martina looked doubtful as Ari flipped through *Star Daze*.

"See? There's all this neat stuff to send away for, and you can read about all these glamorous careers."

"Oh, yeah, those," said Martina. "Did you ever send away for anything?"

"Oh, sure. Sometimes Danny and I would pool our money for something big. But mostly I like to read about learning psychic powers and winning trips to Hollywood and—"

"I never knew you two were so . . ." Martina squinted as though she were peering into Ari's mind. "Is he like your boyfriend?"

"Of *course* not," said Ari, moving away from Martina. "We're just friends."

"But what did you do together? I mean, he's a *boy*!"

"I don't know." Ari folded the corner of the magazine over and over. "We just played together."

"Played? You mean like—*house*?"

"*No!* Y'know, games, like—well, we imagine we're lost somewhere and we have to figure out how to— stay alive. Y'know, survival games." She looked into Martina's eyes and saw that she didn't get it. "Mostly we played Monopoly and swapped comics," she said quickly.

"Oh," chirped Martina. She took up one of the magazines and began flipping through it. "Hey, this looks good," she said. "Let's send away for this."

"What is it?"

"It's a Beauty Extravaganza! It says you get a Bonanza of Beauty Products! Look, you get the first kit free. 'Sparkle with the Spotlight Beauty Kit!' And it's got all this great sparkle makeup."

"What're we going to do with a mess of sparkle makeup? Besides, I've heard that after the first shipment, you have to pay a lot of money every time they send you something." Lydia had warned her about this.

"Then we'll cancel after they send us the free stuff. See? It says, 'Cancel anytime.' And we can use the makeup in school, so our mothers won't find out."

"I don't know," said Ari. Why didn't Martina simply evaporate?

"Oh, don't be such a baby, Ari. It says you can make a Major Beauty Statement. There's 'creamy wands of sparkle color,' and it says it comes with two whole ounces of perfume made from the romantic, mysterious blend of Jasmine, Tuberose, and Oriental Ylang-Ylang Flowers!"

Ari widened her eyes the way Mrs. Atwood did whenever anyone asked, "Can I go to the bathroom?" Mrs. Atwood would always say, "I don't know—*can* you?" Then the person would turn red, realizing that they should've said, "*May* I."

Martina looked up. "This is great, Ari. There's nothing else good in here to send away for." Ari was silent. Martina would never send away for Sea Monkeys or magic potions.

"I'm going to clip this coupon and send it. Give me some scissors." Some power beyond her made Ari go to her desk and hand Martina the scissors. Then she gave Martina an envelope.

"I don't have any stamps," said Ari, and turned away to the business of rearranging the things on her dresser. "And I really don't want to send away for this," she said softly to her hairbrush. Ari looked in the mirror and wished Martina weren't there so she could take off her glasses and become Ruby

Lockheart. She squinted to see if there was any sign that her Bewitchingly Beautiful potion was working, while Martina lay on the floor, busily writing in her own name and address.

"I'll get a stamp at my house," Martina said absently. "And this way it'll come there."

"Fine and dandy with me," Ari said.

They spent the rest of the afternoon playing board games. Bored games is more like it, thought Ari.

As soon as they were in the middle of one game, Martina would be eyeing another box on the shelf. She was like a little kid, only interested in the game that they weren't playing or that she was winning. Ari didn't mind switching games every ten minutes. But she did mind the way Martina just pushed the games away. Ari would be the one left to sort all the cards, dice, and spinners.

"The other night I had the strangest dream," Martina suddenly said. Ari had three men home in Sorry, and she figured this was Martina's way of slowing down her victory.

"A dream?" said Ari.

"Yeah. I had this dream that I told you I was moving away, and you and Tara and Danielle said, 'Wow, that's great!'" Martina studied Ari. Ari kept her eyes down and fiddled with her blue man.

"That's weird," said Ari. "Why would we say that? We would never say that to you."

"Would you be sad if I moved away?" asked Martina. Ari tossed the dice a few times and watched them tumble out of her hands.

"Why would anyone want you to move away?" Ari wished with all her might that Martina had been winning this game.

"Oh, I don't know," said Martina. "Sometimes I think you don't like me. Sometimes I wonder if you say mean things behind my back." She locked eyes with Ari, who just stared at her with pretend surprise. Then Martina said, "Well, lucky for you, I'm not moving away!" She looked down at the board. "Was it my turn or yours? I can't remember. Oops, I think this man of mine was over here," and she moved one of her men closer to home.

When Ari's mother poked her head into the room to tell them that it was getting late, Martina jumped up, leaving Ari with a floorful of dice, chips, and spinners.

"Come for bowling and pizza on Sunday," Martina demanded as she stood at the front door.

"I don't know if I can," said Ari.

"Everyone's going, Ari. Me, Danielle, and Tara. And you gotta bring a boy, okay?"

"A boy?" Ari was incredulous. "What boy are you bringing, Martina?"

"I asked Todd to go with me, and he said yes. It's going to be so much fun, Ari. Like a date. Say yes."

"I don't know . . . maybe. I have to ask my mother."

"Don't tell her about asking a boy," Martina whispered, and comically knocked on Ari's head as if checking for brains. Ari shrugged. She closed the door behind Martina and ran to the phone.

She needed to call Danny. She didn't care if he was pals with the whole U.S. Olympic team, she needed to hear his voice, hear his terrible movie-star impressions, hear about the mega-changes in his new school.

Ari listened to the phone ring twelve times and hung up.

After cleaning her room till there were no traces of Martina left, Ari went to her closet and took out the box that held the gum-wrapper chain. The box was made of unpainted pine, and was so smooth it felt good just to hold it. It was deep and large, like the wardrobe trunks some girls kept their doll things in. That was why her grandmother had given it to her. But Ari had never used it for dolls. She lifted the little brass latch and inhaled the delicious smell. The braid of mint and fruity gum wrappers had been stored inside it for so long that the pine smell had been completely replaced by the aroma of sugary paper. Ari added seven links to the chain and pressed down the latch with a satisfying click. Then she spread out on her bed with *The Weekly Comet* and stared at the ads. But instead of instant escape, she felt an invisible Martina poking at her, prodding at her not to be such a baby. What was this power Martina had? Why did being liked by Martina feel like some kind of weird oxygen Ari couldn't do without?

Maybe Martina is right, she thought. Maybe Martina is perfectly normal, and it's *me* who's weird. Ari's eyes traveled up and down the page of advertisements, and she imagined a picture of Martina, smiling, next to the words *Be a Normal Kid . . . Or Just Look Like One.*

"Danny? Hi, it's me, Ari." She prayed this conversation wouldn't be as disastrous as the last.

"No kidding," said Danny. "I still recognize your voice, y'know."

"Yeah." Ari laughed nervously. "I called before but nobody was there."

"I was at gymnastics. I've been busy with the team."

"I can't believe you're actually on a *team*!"

"Hey, it's not as weird as throwing away my money on a cholesterol count of the stars!"

Ari wished he hadn't remembered that. "Well, the ad *said* it would be celebrities' numbers. Wouldn't *you* think they meant *phone* numbers instead of *cholesterol* numbers?"

"Yeah, well, anyway," Danny continued, "the gymnastics team is a pretty big thing here. A lot of the guys do it." Ari tried to picture Danny in a white tank top and tights, with chalk all over his hands. "So what's been happening with you?"

Ari took a deep breath, trying to remember all the things she wanted to tell him. "Well, (a) I got honorable mention in the dental poster contest, (b) I got kicked out of class during a test all because of the Wallhopper, and (c) I just ate half a box of Pop-Tarts, and, um . . . (d) . . . you wanna . . . um . . . mosey on down to the ole bowling alley on Sunday? There's a group going. We're going to have pizza first." Ari held her breath. The end of her braid made a speedy trip into her mouth.

"Wow, you got kicked out of class?" Danny yelled.

"Yeah," she said, lowering her voice. "I can't talk about it now. I'll tell you on Sunday—okay? Sunday?"

"Just a minute." Danny called to his mother in the background. Ari realized that for the first time, she couldn't visualize where he was or what room he was yelling toward. He came back on the phone. "Yeah, okay," he told her.

After they hung up, Ari stared into the mirror. True, she hadn't been exactly honest with Danny.

She had carefully left out the part about it being like a date, and he probably figured it was just like it used to be—Ari and Danny, only with a bunch of other kids. Ari suddenly felt angry. Stop being so weird, she thought. She yanked out the elastic holding her braid, pulled the wavy sections apart, and pushed her hair in front of her shoulders.

"Well, at least you could try and *look* like a normal kid," she whispered.

Chapter

12

"I'm scorekeeper!" shouted Philip.

"Me too!" yelled Todd.

"No fair," whined Danielle. "We need one girl and one boy." Danny and Ari shared a look. Danielle was infuriatingly fair.

"Okay, but I get to choose," said Todd, "and I choose . . . Ari." Ari sat down at the desk and took up the stubby yellow pencil. Martina had formed the teams: Martina, Todd, Tara, and Philip on one team; Ari, Danny, Danielle, and Joel on the other. They took turns, cheering or groaning, depending on the outcome at the end of each frame. Somewhere in the middle of the second game, everyone started to lose interest. Martina spent most of the time dashing in and out of the bathroom with Tara, while Philip and Danny kept running to the vending machines. Ari had just about filled up her half of the score sheet with doodles when Martina emerged from the bathroom with an idea.

"Let's play another game, but this time we'll divide into couples. Me and Todd, Tara and Joel, Danielle and Philip, and Ari and Danny." Then Martina giggled her munchkin laugh, and everyone looked embarrassed. Ari's heart raced as she looked over at Danny. He looked as though he had a bad taste in his mouth. Then his eyes found Ari's and silently asked her: "Did you know about this?"

Ari didn't have time to wipe the guilty look off her face, and she knew Danny felt tricked. He gave her a swift "Boy, have you changed" look, grabbed his jacket, and said, "I'm outta here. I gotta go. See ya, guys." All heads followed him as he plunked down some damp, balled-up dollar bills, leapt up the steps, and ran out of the Bowl-a-Rama.

"Ari, did you two have a fight?" Martina asked in a motherly voice.

Ari glared at her. "Forget it, Martina," she replied stiffly.

"Well, if Danny's going, I don't want to hang around either," whined Philip. He turned to Todd and Joel. "You wanna play some pinball?"

"Yeah," said Joel, already pulling off his shoes. "And then we can go to Todd's. He's got a new computer game."

"My house?" said Todd. He looked at Martina and shook his blond hair out of his eyes. Then he glanced back at Joel and Philip tying their sneakers and shrugged helplessly at her.

As soon as Todd, Joel, and Philip left, Martina brushed them off with her "Boys—what can you do?" look. "I was tired of bowling anyway," she said. "Let's go to Fendell's!"

Ari brightened at the idea. Fendell's drugstore was huge and smelled like new toys. Ari loved it because you could spend all day thumbing through the magazines, and no one ever bothered you.

Martina flew up and down the aisles of the store, yelling, "I've got that! I've got that!" and slapping at the packages as if they were being tagged It. "Let's go look at the makeup!" They all followed her. Ari felt so powerful running up and down the aisles in a small herd that she almost forgot about Danny. Occasionally, Danielle and Tara would point out the brands their mothers or older sisters used.

"My sister never uses this makeup," Ari declared.

"Never?" Danielle asked, incredulous.

"Almost never," answered Ari.

"Yeah, but your sister's kind of weird, isn't she?" said Martina.

"I don't know," said Ari, feeling strangely protective of Lydia. "She and her friends hardly ever wear makeup. And when they do, they only use the organic kind. They say most of the stuff here hurts animals."

"I never saw animals with makeup," Tara said, hands on hips. Ari couldn't help laughing out loud.

"In the labs where they make the stuff!" she shouted in Tara's face. Tara looked confused. "They experiment with different formulas to see which ones might be harmful to people. They put drops of chemicals on a rabbit's skin and in its eyes. If it blinds the rabbit or burns its skin, they go back to the drawing board."

"Oh, gross," commented Danielle.

"Aw, de paw widdow wabbit," teased Martina. "My mother says that not all these companies use animals."

Tara and Danielle widened their eyes at Ari as if to say, "See? Martina *does* know everything."

"Besides," Martina whispered, leaning in close to all of them, "look what I got—and it's not for any stupid rabbit!"

She opened her pink parka and revealed the top of a lipstick package sticking out of an inner pocket. Tara, Danielle, and Ari stared at her as though she had just hypnotized them. "Go on, get something," urged Martina. "Then we can all share it." Tara and

Danielle giggled and looked nervously at Martina. Ari watched them intently, unsure what she should do. Tara and Danielle silently searched each other's eyes.

"What are you—chicken?" The girls considered that for a moment, so Martina tried a gentler tack. "C'mon, it's easy. I just picked it up like any other person in this store and put it in here." She patted her pocket. Tara and Danielle turned to each other for a reaction. "Look," said Martina, impatient, "we have as much right to pick up the stuff in this store as anyone else. Danielle, there's a hot-pink eye shadow over there. And there's a popcorn lip gloss down there, Tara. Go get it."

Like obedient dogs, Tara and Danielle slowly walked in opposite directions, eyeing the abundant racks. Ari just stayed near Martina, who was casually perusing the cosmetics, asking Ari her opinion of this one and that one, as if she really cared to know what Ari thought. Ari felt like Erica Finn, intruding on a game she didn't understand. She wanted to take off and run home the way Erica had, but then Martina would think she was a baby who couldn't follow the rules.

Soon Danielle and Tara returned and quickly flashed their loot. Ari's hands turned cold and clammy. The girls were huddled close together, with Martina's face so close to Ari's that she was practically a blur. Ari felt Martina's sharp bubble-gum breath shoot up her nose as Martina hissed, "Get something!"

Ari stood still. It was as if Martina had cast a spell on her that made it impossible for her to move. Danielle nudged her, and she almost fell over. Stumbling over her own feet, Ari turned and walked away from them, wishing there were a black hole at the end of the aisle into which she could simply vanish.

Keeping her eyes front, Ari decided to just continue walking, but at the last second she heard them whispering. She shot her arm out stiffly, like a toy soldier, and grabbed the first thing she touched. She didn't even look to see what she had grabbed, because her yanking had caused several other packages to fall off the display. The shaking rack hurled lipsticks, blushers, powders, and brushes off their hooks and smacked them to the floor. Ari heard the shrieks from the girls at the other end of the aisle and looked to see if they would help her. But in a flash they had disappeared. Ari fell to her knees and began fitting the tiny holes of the packages onto any hook that would accept them.

A woman walked over to her.

"Can I help you find something?" she asked sternly. Ari felt all the blood rush to her face.

"No, thank you," she murmured. Could the

woman see how much her hands were trembling? The woman took her time walking past her, and Ari could feel her watching. When Ari had finished cleaning up, she stuck her sweaty, shaking hands into her pockets and strode out of Fendell's as fast as she could without actually running.

Once outside, however, she broke into a sprint and ran through the darkening streets, over the railroad tracks, past the library, and up the hill to her block. As she ran, panting, a harsh dryness burned in her throat and an unbearable stabbing pain pierced her right below the ribs. She grabbed her side. It was the same sharp pain she felt whenever their gym teacher made them run laps around the ball field. But this time she didn't want to give in to it, didn't want to stop until she ran out of sidewalk. Tripping on the steps to her house, she slapped down hard on her hands to break her fall. She felt the scrapes burned into her palms by the gritty planks, but she didn't stop. She just wanted to get inside.

As Ari stood in the upstairs bathroom with her coat on and her hands under cold water, she listened to the drone of the television in her parents' room. Lydia was home. Ari threw cup after cup of water down her throat, then gently patted her sore hands dry and went to her room. The pain in her side was almost gone, but her heart still raced. She lay down on her bed and felt the drum pulsing through her body. She hugged her pillow to make it stop.

When the pounding subsided, a picture of Danny, angry and running away from her, filled the screen in Ari's mind. The voice from the screen yelled, "Friendships Don't Die—You Kill Them!" Ari sat up.

"Stop that!" she said aloud, wiping the tears from her eyes. What a time for her mind to come up with snappy slogans!

Ari got up and looked for something to blow her nose with. She shook some crumbs off a napkin from yesterday's snack and wiped her nose. Then she took off her glasses and examined her blotchy red face in the mirror. How come people in the movies and on TV never looked so lousy when they cried? Ari suddenly was reminded of her grandfather's funeral, where all the grown-ups were hugging and honking into their handkerchiefs. Her aunt Barbara was a wreck. When she had come over and put her arms around Ari, she had wanted to pull away. It didn't look like pretty Aunt Barbara. On TV and in the movies nobody looked so bad that you'd want to run away from them. If I'm ever an aunt at a funeral, thought Ari, I'll wear special makeup so that I won't scare my niece or nephew.

Makeup: The word made her stomach feel oogy and brought back the bubble-gum breath and cold stare of Martina, daring Ari to steal and become one of them. Did Ari want to? Not really. But Martina was always so sure of herself, and she liked Ari, so wasn't that better than being alone? Ari felt as though she were in a maze, with no idea which way would lead her out and which way would only lead her deeper into confusion.

She was still wearing her coat, and when she unzipped it she heard something fall to the floor. She looked down and saw a small package of lip gloss. She picked it up: Violet Caprice. Somehow, in the panic to put all those packages back, this had fallen into her jacket.

Well, it's here, thought Ari, and there's nothing I can do about that. She punched open the package, and with her hand still shaking a bit, she smeared some Violet Caprice on her lips. Then she brought her face up to the mirror till her lips almost touched the glass. Her mouth looked as though it had been shoved into a vat of dark purple Vaseline. It had a sickly sweet grapey smell that made you want to taste it, but when she licked her lips, all she got was a blob of flavorless petroleum jelly.

"Yilch!" Ari ran the back of her hand across her lips and tongue. Then, looking back at herself in the mirror, she decided that Violet Caprice might not look half bad if, perhaps, she were also wearing violet contact lenses with micro sparkle points. It was definitely worth holding on to. Just to see.

Ari looked around her room for a decent hiding place for the lipstick, but no spot was truly foolproof against an inquisitive dustrag or the hands that tucked clean laundry into her drawers.

What am I going to do with you? she thought, suddenly feeling trapped by the two-inch container of purple gook. She didn't want to throw it away. Besides, Lydia and her mother shared an uncanny ability to detect incriminating garbage.

Then Ari remembered the secret book safe she had once sent away for. She pulled it out of her bookshelf. Until now, there had been nothing truly worthy of hiding in such a secret place. Ari opened the front cover of the book. Instead of pages, there was a piece of cardboard that covered a hollow space to put things in. Ari dropped the Violet Caprice into the space, then wedged the book in between *Charlotte's Web*, one of her favorites, and *Wuthering Heights*, which she had never read but liked because it made her bookshelf look more grown-up.

Feeling as clever and furtive as a spy, Ari went back to the bathroom, splashed some cold water on her face, and ran downstairs. She would apologize to Danny, and everything would go back to the way it was. But by the time Ari reached the kitchen, her determination had strangely disappeared. She started dialing but hung up the phone. Back in her room, she picked up the Magic Eight Ball key chain. She asked: "Is Danny still my friend?" and turned it over for the answer: Reply Hazy. Try Again. She tossed the Eight Ball on her bed.

That evening, Lydia stood in front of the refrigerator with both the refrigerator and freezer doors open. Their parents were attending a concert, so Lydia and Ari were alone.

Good, thought Ari. No third degree on the bowling till morning.

"So whaddya want for supper?" asked Lydia. "Pizza, eggrolls— What's this?" Her arms reached deep into the freezer and pulled out a pile of foil-wrapped packages. "God, I wish Mom would mark these. There's a whole bunch of these frozen bricks. Look at this one—it's a perfect trapezoid! Who in the world has trapezoidal food?"

Ari sat on the counter, softly kicking the cabinets below with her heels, watching Lydia as if she were TV.

Normally Ari enjoyed *The Lydia Show* and their evenings alone. The air was different without their parents. She felt freer, somehow. As Ari watched and kicked, Lydia continued her excavation of the freezer. Then Lydia put some frozen egg rolls into the toaster oven and waited for Ari to argue with her. When she didn't say anything, Lydia studied her a little more closely. "So, how was bowling with your little friends?"

"They're *not* my little friends," said Ari, kicking the cabinets harder. "If I had gone bowling with a group of *munchkins*, then *they* would be my *little friends*."

"Oh, okay," Lydia said carefully. "So . . . how was it?"

"So-so. I got two spares and a strike."

"I mean who was there, dummy?"

"Some kids from school."

"Duh, no kidding. Could you be more specific?"

"Oh, I don't know. Martina, Tara, Danielle . . . some others, too."

Lydia's face brightened, and she hoisted her backside onto the kitchen table, eager to hear more. "That's great. See, I knew when Danny moved you'd widen your circle a little." Ari looked back at her darkly. "Y'know," continued Lydia, "my environment group was thinking of creating a sort of junior club, y'know, so kids your age could learn about what we're doing to help the environment. Then maybe your group could take off on its own. Why don't you ask your friends to come to our next meeting, and then, y'know, you could start your own little club."

Ari jumped down from the counter, glaring at Lydia. "Oh, jeepers, could we, Lydia? And what should we call our *little club*—Save the Guppies? Sor-ry, but no one's joining any *little club*. You think those creeps care about the environment? That's a good one!" Ari felt her whole body quivering. She had to get out from under Lydia's watchful gaze. "That's a real good one!" she shouted, and ran upstairs.

Huddled in her reading niche, Ari found no comfort, even with the latest issue of *Star Daze*. When the grumbling in her stomach grew unbearable, she quickly went downstairs to sneak some Pop-Tarts back up to her room. Nibbling the bland, crusty edges first, she thought of Danny and his four food groups. He would assure her that Pop-Tarts were just fine for supper because if you really thought about it, the crust fell into the cereals and grains group, and the jam, well, jam was just boiled fruit. A glass of milk for dairy, and you were all set.

Ari went into her parents' room, settled back into the millions of pillows on their bed, and turned on the video player. The tape inside was most of the way through *The Wizard of Oz*. Dorothy, with her fancy Emerald City hairdo, was trapped in the castle of the Wicked Witch of the West. Sobbing, Dorothy confided to the crystal ball: "Auntie Em, I'm frightened! I'm frightened!" For a moment the gray, soft face of Auntie Em appeared in the crystal ball, comforting Dorothy with her familiar creaky voice. But a second later Auntie Em's face dissolved into a gray blur and was replaced by the green face of the Wicked Witch of the West.

Ari stopped eating and sat forward, fascinated. She'd seen it a million times, and when she was little, the sight of that scary green face filling the screen and pressing itself right into the audience had always made her burst into uncontrollable sobbing. She would run into the bathroom and press her eyes against the towel bar and stand there until the gush of tears subsided. Her family didn't know whether to laugh because it was cute or be concerned that she was so terrified.

Lydia popped her head in. "Auntie Em! Auntie Em!" she cackled, waiting for Ari to laugh. But Ari just kept on watching. "Better not leave any crumbs in their bed," Lydia said flatly, and closed the door.

Dorothy made it to Oz and almost all the way back home without Ari shedding a tear. Then the moment came for Dorothy to say good-bye to her friends, and Ari felt her throat tighten and her cheeks grow hot. She had never choked up during this part before. As Dorothy dabbed the eyes of the

Cowardly Lion and cautioned the Tin Man against rusting, Ari felt hot tears push up, and the screen went blurry. Dorothy faced the Scarecrow with his kind, triangular eyes and his saggy smile, and Ari bit down hard on her lower lip.

She pressed one of the small pillows against her eyes as hard as she could and held it there through Dorothy's return to her gray little bedroom and while the credits crept up the screen. Exhausted, Ari fell back against the pillows and lay watching the static for a while.

When Ari's parents came home, Ari was awake in her own bed with the lights out. Lying with her back to her door, she felt the hallway light spread over her as her mother walked in and sat on the edge of her bed. Ari pretended to be asleep and was surprised that her mother sat there watching her for a minute.

"Good night, sweetie," her mother whispered, and lightly kissed the back of Ari's head. She closed the door almost all the way, leaving just a crack of light—the way Ari liked it.

Listening to the comforting sounds of her mother and father moving between their bedroom and the bathroom, she first heard the *click-click* of heels, followed by the soft shuffle of slippers. Then the water running, the toilet flushing, her mother murmuring about the new exhibition she'd just finished mounting.

Her life is so easy, thought Ari. No one hands her nasty notes or tells her that her clothes are all wrong or what she should be like. Her friends don't leave her just like that.

Ari punched the sides of her pillow and tried to get comfortable.

"Now, lookit, Ari," a voice inside her said, "you ain't usin' your head about this. Think you didn't have any brains."

"I have so got brains!"

"Then why don't you use 'em?"

Ari tossed and grunted. Her body felt heavy with exhaustion, but she just couldn't fall asleep. She bit the corner of her pillow and cursed Danny. "Damn you for leaving," she whispered. "You messed up everything."

Chapter

13

The next morning Mrs. Zwort announced that Mrs. Atwood wouldn't be back in school until the following week. Ari couldn't believe it. The Zwort just wouldn't go away. Already more than half the class had their names on the board, and Ari wondered what the Zwort would do when she ran out of space for all her annoying little check marks.

Peter Martindale was having a ball with the name Ara-idne. It was as if someone had handed him a new slingshot. Ari was sick of it, and with the Zwort there for another week, she really didn't care if she got into trouble. The next time he sailed by her with his big, goofy smile and asked, "How's your kidney, Ara-idne?" she'd punch him in the face. He deserved it. So did Martina, for that matter. Yesterday's disaster at the drugstore plus her late night had left Ari tired, grouchy, and ready to strike out at the next person who ticked her off.

"Girls, stop conjugating in the doorway," said Mrs. Zwort in her prickly voice. Martina rolled her eyes, and Hannah looked at Ari with her hand over her smiling mouth.

"Doesn't she mean congregating?" said Hannah.

"I don't know," said Ari. "Maybe she thinks we're standing here *conjugating*." Hannah giggled, but Martina looked impatient with them.

"That's right, like: 'I talk, you talk, he, she, or it talks!'" Hannah laughed and nodded toward the Zwort.

"Righto," Ari snickered.

"Hannah, what are you talking about?" Martina sneered.

"Get it?" said Ari. "Conjugating in the doorway? Like conjugating verbs?"

Martina gave a weak laugh. "So, Ari," she said, ignoring both Hannah and the Zwort, "you missed all the fun. Y'know, after you left." Martina widened her eyes to show she was speaking in code. "We went to Tara's and had hot cocoa and tried on all the you-know-what. Boy, you really botched it at Fendell's! You looked so stupid when all that stuff went flying!" Martina laughed and laughed, frantically waving her hands around in a reenactment of

Ari's panicky bungle. Hannah looked down at her feet and then at Ari. "But that's okay, Ari." Martina smiled. "I'll still let you come over to my house and borrow the stuff I got."

Ari stood frozen between Hannah and Martina's gaze. She didn't know what to say.

"Girls!" Mrs. Zwort was getting mad, and soon her check marks would have to spill over onto the blackboard next door. Hannah had started walking back toward her desk when Mrs. Zwort held out the attendance sheet toward her. "Miss Swensen, would you take this down to the office, please?"

Martina pulled Ari back into the doorway and, putting her arm through Ari's, crooned in her ear so close that Ari could smell the honeyed scent of her flowery shampoo, "Yes, Little Miss Perfect, why don't you take the attendance sheet? You're the only one in this class who can be trusted."

Martina looked at Ari for agreement, but Ari pulled her arm out from Martina's grasp and crooned back to her, "Martina: Shut up." Martina's eyes narrowed down to the meanest little slits she could manage. She flipped back a piece of her perfectly smooth, shiny hair.

"Oh, so now you're pals with that teacher's pet? Ari, believe me, it doesn't work. Getting chummy with Hannah isn't going to make you teacher's pet too. Not by a long shot."

"That isn't what I think, and you don't have to go picking on Hannah just because she's the way she is."

"Oh, fine," answered Martina. She nudged Ari hard on the way back to her seat, and turned around and mouthed the word *X-Friend* at her before sitting down.

Ari stumbled to her seat, amazed that in only a few short seconds she had managed to wreck her entire life. She opened her journal, which was filled with pages of one line entries stating the weather and the contents of her lunch box. But today she couldn't help it, she needed to speak to Mrs. Atwood even if she wasn't here.

She turned to a fresh page and wrote her usual: *Sunny, cold, with salami and grapes.* Then beneath it: *Everything's changed. Nothing fits anymore and it stinks.*

At recess Ari noticed Martina dramatically whispering to Tara and Danielle and turning to glare at her every few seconds. Ari was throwing her Super Pinkie ball hard against the side of the school, and when she thought of Martina, she threw it so hard it flew over her head and rolled toward the girls turning two jump ropes for Clarinda Pallaster. Ari forgot her ball for a moment and stopped to watch Clarinda hop and twirl through the bobbing ropes.

Clarinda's feet seemed independent of the rest of her body, and her arms were loose and wavy, as if they didn't have a care in the world. As the ropes slapped the pavement, the girls' hands moved in tandem with Clarinda's feet, their soft voices chanting, counting out the jumps in their double-Dutch trance. Sometimes Clarinda would close her eyes for a moment, as though the ropes' rhythmic *slap whoop, slap whoop* had carried her far away to some other place. When the ball rolled against Clarinda's feet, the ropes sagged to a stop and fell limp in the turners' hands. Ari rushed over, apologizing. Clarinda untangled the ropes around her feet and stepped out to hand her the ball.

"Thanks," said Ari. She noticed how Clarinda's eyes rolled toward Martina, then back to Ari. Clarinda's gaze traveled up and down Ari, inspecting her.

"You wanna turn the ropes?" Clarinda asked. For a split second Ari wanted nothing more than to drop the ball and spend the rest of her natural life turning the ropes for Clarinda. But then Ari glanced back at Martina, who caught her eye. She felt her stomach pretzel with fear.

"Thanks," Ari said, smiling. "Maybe tomorrow."

Clarinda nodded, then glanced once more at Martina and her little group. "It's none of my business, but you shouldn't hang around that girl. She messes with your head so she can boss you around. She's already done it with those two, and now she's trying to build up her little army, if you know what I mean."

"Yeah, I do now," Ari said, bouncing her ball. "Well, I gotta go." And she watched Clarinda as she twisted away and leapt back into the undulating ropes.

When the bell rang, Tara and Danielle rushed up to Ari. "You shouldn't have said what you said," Danielle told Ari.

"Yeah," Tara chimed in. "It really hurt Martina's feelings." Ari was dumbfounded.

"I sure wouldn't want to be you," said Danielle, and Tara nodded in agreement. Together they flung themselves through the school doors.

That afternoon Martina began her campaign to show Ari just how she handled an X-Friend. During art class, Martina "accidentally" knocked the jar of water with the paintbrushes into Ari's lap. Ari leapt up just in time to miss soaking her pants, but her sneakers got it, and for the rest of the day her chilled feet in wet shoes made a strange *thwack*ing sound as she walked. On the way out of music class, Ari tripped over someone's foot and nearly fell flat on her face. When she looked up she saw Martina quickly dashing away, calling, "Tara! Wait up!"

Hannah Swensen stooped down to help her pick

up her books. "It was Martina," she said, tucking a piece of her hair behind her ear.

Ari blew on her sore palms, trying to cool them off. "I know," she said, trying to look as if she didn't mind.

"Do you want me to go with you to tell someone?"

"Nah. Just 'cause I've got a wicked witch mad at me doesn't mean you have to get into this mess." Ari stood up and brushed off her pants at the knees.

Hannah stood up with her, furrowed her brow for a moment, and then leaned in comically toward Ari. " 'I'm not afraid of witches!' " she said, now widening her eyes. " 'In fact, I'm not afraid of anything—except for a lighted match, that is.' " She grabbed at a piece of her sweater and shook it a little.

" 'Well, I don't blame you for that!' " Ari answered, really smiling for the first time that day. She offered Hannah her arm. " 'To Oz?' " Hannah hooked her arm into Ari's.

" '*To Oz!*' " shouted Hannah, then quickly covered her mouth. Both girls burst out laughing as they ran to catch up with the rest of the class.

Chapter

14

Ari was setting the table for supper, looking up at the doorway now and then to check that her mother and father were safely absorbed in whatever they were doing. When she had finished placing all the glasses directly over the knives, she hooked her right thumb into her back pocket. It was still there.

Her father came sauntering into the kitchen, his hand deep in a box of crackers. He looked like a little kid caught with his hand in the cookie jar.

"Daddy," said Ari, "aren't you supposed to cut down on that stuff? Those are loaded with salt."

Her father pulled his hand out of the box and licked the grease and salt off his fingertips. "I am, I am."

She smiled at him and closed the box just to be

sure. "I thought Mom got some health chips, anyway. She had a whole bowl of them in the living room."

"Wood chips, you mean," said her father, making a sour face.

Ari opened the refrigerator. "Well, I won't tell on you—this time," she said, pulling soda bottles out of the refrigerator. Then, as soon as he had left the room, she heard a familiar rustling and saw that the cracker box was gone.

"I can hear you!" she called, and poured the soda into four glasses. Then she reached into her back pocket for the tiny bottle marked PASSION. She had just poured two drops of the potion into Lydia's drink when she heard the front door open. Lydia was back from her meeting.

"Mom!" Lydia's voice was muffled, but she sounded panicky. Ari ran out to the hallway. Lydia stood in the middle of the hall, her blue scarf wrapped around half her face and her eyes bugging out.

"God, Lydia, I didn't think it was that cold out."

"Where's Mom?"

"Mo-o-om!" Ari yelled, and soon their mother came downstairs in her robe and slippers. On work days, after her glass of wine, she always changed into her comfy clothes.

"Lydia, why are you standing there like that?" She

sounded annoyed. "What's going on?" Lydia pulled her scarf down, and now Ari and her mother were the ones with the bug eyes. Lydia's cheeks were swollen and covered with a bumpy rash that made her look a little like Waldo the Walrus.

"Oh my God, Lydia!" exclaimed Mrs. Spire. "What happened? Are you sick? Where did this rash come from?" Mrs. Spire circled Lydia as if she were some rare species of daughter that she had never before encountered.

Mr. Spire came out of his study, and as soon as he saw Lydia, his eyes bugged out like a cartoon dad's. "Lydia, what happened?"

"I don't know," croaked Lydia. Tears came streaming down her cheeks. "When I woke up this morning," she sniffed, "my face felt kind of tingly, but I figured it was just chapped. So I put some cream on. But then in school, it started itching a little, so I washed it with cold water. I didn't even use any soap. Then it was okay for a while, I guess, but during our ecology meeting, it started tingling again, and then someone said they thought I was coming down with the mumps or something. It itches like crazy!"

"Don't scratch!" her parents shrieked in unison.

"It can't be the mumps," said Mr. Spire. "You've had all the shots. Um . . . did you ever have the chicken pox?"

"Of *course* she's had the *chicken* pox!" said Mrs. Spire, exasperated. "Don't you remember, we were all set to go to Disney World . . ." She stopped speaking and cranked her hand in lieu of finishing the story. The memory of Lydia getting chicken pox the day of their Disney vacation was always too painful for the girls to relive.

Mr. Spire sighed. "Could it have been something you touched in chemistry class?" he asked.

"I take biology."

"Is it on any other part of your body?"

Lydia shook her head.

"Was it something you ate?" As soon as the words came out of Mrs. Spire's mouth, Ari's heart started pounding.

"I don't think so." Lydia bit her bottom lip in a concentrated effort to remember everything she had put in her mouth for the past twenty-four hours. "No," she said, "I haven't eaten anything I don't usually eat."

Ari bit the inside of her cheek. Two small drops of Passion over the past two weeks had indeed made a startling change in her sister. Only instead of making her the object of teenage romance, it had made Lydia look more like her beloved walruses!

"Wait a minute," said Ari's mother. "You've had this before. Don't you remember? Strawberries!

This is exactly what happened when you had strawberries last summer. It's an allergic reaction, and see? The swelling is going down already."

"But I didn't eat any strawberries," sniffed Lydia.

"Well, something you ate must be having the same effect," said her father. "Let's think what you could've eaten: strawberries, raspberries—"

"Magic potions," squeaked Ari. All heads turned to her.

"What?" said her family all at once. Ari swallowed. It was as if her heart were lodged in her throat and throbbing so hard it was difficult to speak.

"A magic potion," Ari said, tossing off the words lightly in the hope that she wouldn't have to explain and they would all just nod in understanding. No one nodded.

"Ari," her father began, "what do you mean by magic potion? You didn't slip your sister some eye of newt or lizard's tongue—did you?"

Ari shook her head. "No, that was the Witch's Brew Kit, and it never really worked, anyway. It was just a bunch of dry seaweed."

"Would somebody please tell me what this little creep did that made me break out in this rash?" cried Lydia.

"Yes. Tell us everything, Ari," said her mother.

"Well." Ari gulped. "I only put in a little bit, and I know it's not poison or anything because the label said—"

"The label? What label?" asked Ari's father.

"The label on the Passion potion." Now Ari's family was gaping at her as if it were she, not Lydia, who had something very wrong with her.

"*Passion potion?* Ari, bring it here. Right now," said her mother.

Ari reached into her back pocket and handed her father the bottle of Passion. He read the tiny print on the label: " 'All-Natural Strawberry Extract.' Well, at least we know that's all it is," he said with a sigh of relief. He put his arm around Lydia. "That rash will be gone very soon. It doesn't look nearly as angry as it did just a few minutes ago."

Ari smiled weakly at Lydia, but even though her rash didn't look angry, Lydia sure did.

"Ari, why on *earth* were you giving Lydia a passion potion?" asked her mother.

"It was kind of an experiment," Ari answered. "I only wanted to help! I wanted to see if it would help Lydia fall in love with someone."

"You little twerp!" snapped Lydia. "I'm going to kill you—"

"I'm really sorry!" yelled Ari, and before her family could see the tears, she ran to her room and slammed the door.

Tucked into her reading niche, Ari hugged her knees and waited. Great, she thought. First I get kicked out of class, then I'm stealing lipsticks, and now this. Tomorrow they'll probably send me to one of those Rotten Kid schools hidden away in the mountains, where they wake you up in the middle of the night to run you around a ball field and put you in solitary confinement for not making your bed right.

Ari listened to the mumbling sounds of her parents and Lydia downstairs, then the footsteps on the stairs, the bottles being emptied into the toilet, and finally the incriminating *clink* of tiny glass bottles in the bathroom wastebasket. When the clinking stopped and the toilet flushed, Ari's stomach lurched. Her mother and her father came into her room and made her come out of her reading niche.

"Ari," her mother began, "do you realize how *dangerous* and *stupid* this little experiment of yours was?" The word *stupid* hung in the air and stung Ari like a slap in the face. "You just can't go sneaking around, slipping people magic potions without their permission. And of all people, *Lydia* does not need a passion potion. Believe me, she's got plenty of passion."

Ari knit her eyebrows. What were they saying? There were no dates, no love notes falling out of coat pockets, no phone calls from boys, if you didn't count boys like Lydia's pal Andrew Puno, and Ari certainly didn't. There was just Lydia and her usual gang. "*Lydia* has passion?"

"Of course Lydia has passion," said her father. "Haven't you been in her room lately?"

"Sure," said Ari. "It's full of posters of rain forests and pimply walruses."

"Exactly," said her mother. "Lydia is very passionate about all her environment projects."

"I thought passion meant romantic stuff," said Ari meekly.

"Passion is not just romantic stuff," said her mother. "It's also whatever makes you feel *alive* and *excited*, the things that give you *joy*, or the things you *feel* very strongly about." The way her mother spoke about passion made Ari's own heart beat fast. And she had to admit, if that was what passion could be, her sister certainly had it.

"Is Lydia going to be all right?" asked Ari.

"She's going to be fine," answered her father. "You, however, may not be your sister's favorite person right now. If I were you, I'd start working on a mighty impressive apology."

"And there won't be any allowance for a while," added her mother. "That should put a crimp in your purchasing power."

When her parents had left the room, Ari sat thinking about passion. She had never really connected the word with people she knew, and yet everyone in her family had it: Her father was passionate about ancient civilizations, her mother was passionate about art—and cooking. Even Ari had her passions. Maybe, she thought, that was what she loved about the characters in her favorite old movies; they were always so passionate.

Ari wanted to run downstairs and call Danny to tell him about the potions and how they really worked—sort of. But after Martina's bowling party, she was afraid he'd never speak to her again.

She opened up a magazine and stared at the ad for Cassandra's Oracles. Except for the stupid part about babies, Cassandra really had seen Ari's future. Martina *had* gotten close to Ari, but now Ari was miserable. And no allowance meant financial hardship for sure. She got up and pulled out her knit hat, where she had been saving for the contact lenses with micro sparkle points. A few quarters jingled sadly. Nearly her entire savings had been forked over when her parents discovered the call to Cassandra on the phone bill.

I'll be eighty thousand years old by the time I have enough for those lenses, Ari thought. But she wouldn't give up. If magic potions couldn't change things, there was always passion. Other people held on to their passions, and so would Ari Spire.

Chapter

15

"I'm glad I'm in your group," Hannah told Ari the next day as they walked to their classroom. Ari had pulled one mitten off with her mouth, and it was still dangling there as she shrugged off her sagging backpack.

"Whuff group?" she muttered through a mouthful of polar fleece.

"For our mythology projects," said Hannah. "Don't you remember Mrs. Zwort saying that Mrs. Atwood would be back at the end of the week?" Ari dropped the mitten out of her mouth and stuffed it into her pocket.

"She is?" Where had she been when the Zwort told them that?

Hannah nodded. "And apparently she gave Mrs.

Zwort the groups for the projects. She said we have to take mythology books out today at the library." Ari stared at her slushy boots. She had to stop daydreaming in class so much, even if it did mean listening to the Zwort.

"Who elsc is in our group?"

"You, me, and Clarinda." Hannah tucked away the hair that was always falling in her face. It was like a twitch with her, the way she brought her right hand up every few seconds and swished it by the side of her narrow face. Now she came to a full stop and whispered, "I have a sneaking suspicion that we're going to have a lot of work on our hands. Clarinda's in a new ballet and always flying off to rehearsals."

"True," said Ari, "but don't you worry. We've got Mithter Myth on our side."

"Who?"

"My father! He was practically raised on Mount Olympus." Ari started walking backward to avoid the view of the approaching classroom door. The idea of seeing the Zwort and Martina in one room was more than Ari could bear.

Every day Mrs. Zwort handed out a thick pile of crossword puzzles and word searches to keep the class busy. But Martina was already busy finding ways to let Ari know that she wasn't going to easily forget the words *shut up*.

That afternoon she brushed Ari's cheek with an indelible Magic Marker. The next day she spilled her milk into her lunch, pushed it all over to Ari's place, and complained loudly to the lunchroom monitor about the mess on her table. On Friday after gym Martina stood in line with her fingers pinching her nose and whined, "Pee-yew, someone stinks— Oh, it's you, Ari!" Danielle and Tara always stood by Martina snickering, and by now the boys were quietly rooting for a fight.

"You gonna beat her up after school?" asked Peter Martindale. He leaned over the entire surface of his desk, smiling so broadly that for the first time Ari thought he was on her side.

"She's testing you," confided Hannah as they put away their books for the day. "She wants to see what you'll do." Hannah's anxious face seemed to ask the same question. Ari wished Hannah could tell her what to do, but when it came to Martina, even 5A's best student was stumped.

"I don't know what to do," whispered Ari. "Really, I just want to go home."

Hannah put on her best Glinda voice: "You've always had the power to go home, my dear. You just click your heels two times—"

"Three times," said Ari absently. She was looking around the room for Martina.

Before school ended, Ari took out her journal,

turned to a fresh sheet, and pressed the binding so it would lie flat. Mrs. Atwood would be back on Monday, and Ari felt she should record something besides it being partly cloudy with bologna and cheese.

M.A.: I'm glad you're back. Ari looked at the words and felt something gnawing inside her. Well, of course, she'd be glad to have Mrs. Atwood back; but thoughts of the past two weeks were stirring around and around, till all her confusion and loneliness were whisked to the top in a thick, angry froth. Ari needed to dish it out.

I think it's really lousy when a teacher leaves their class for two whole weeks with the worst substitute in the entire galaxy, especially when some people might be having the worst weeks of their entire life. Some kids thought you might be dead, but I figured you were just sick of teaching and went to live on a tropical island and drink out of coconut shells all day or something. I know how you always like us to give details in our writing, so I will tell you that Mrs. Zwort wears perfume that smells like bathroom air freshener and sits at your desk looking like a constipated toad. She hates kids and is using up all your chalk. She's mean and stupid, and all she ever does is read The Enquirer *and yell at us.*

Aren't you glad to know we learned nothing at all?

Ari looked over the words that had erupted over the page. It was good, but she wasn't completely satisfied. If Mrs. Atwood had been there, Ari wouldn't have felt so blurry. She would've known how to handle Martina's poisonous friendship, and she wouldn't be sitting in a classroom full of kids licking their chops for a schoolyard fight. Ari took up her pen. *By the way, Mrs. Zwort says that drinking coffee in class is* very *unprofessional.*

It certainly wasn't the best slam, but it would do. Ari slapped her journal closed and put it with the others piled on the teacher's desk.

The dismissal bell rang, and as kids moved into the hall, Ari felt all faces turn to her. Even the Dingles looked interested.

"Y'want me to walk you home?" asked Brian Tucker.

"Why would I want you to do that?"

"Don't know." Brian shrugged, stuffing all the papers that had ripped at the holes back into his binder. "Just thought you might want some help if things get messy with the Wallhopper."

"Nothing's going to get messy, and I know how to find my way home." Ari gave a tug at her jacket zipper and strode out of the cloakroom, attempting her best Lydia face. Neck stretched, chin up, teeth clenched.

Outside, the mass of kids broke into its usual little bunches and scattered away from the school. Ari was miffed that Hannah had a dentist appointment. And as usual, Clarinda had dance class. Ari had wanted to invite someone over so that she wouldn't be alone for the walk home. She kept company with the little clouds that puffed out as she breathed, and as she started down the hilly street, she heard laughter behind her. Without even turning around, she knew it was Tara and Danielle. Martina, thank God, lived in the opposite direction.

"Say, Ari, what're you going to do after school today?" whined Tara. "Can I come over and play house?" The two girls giggled.

"No, no, you can't play with her," Danielle joined in. "She only plays with her boyfriend, Danny. Say, Ari, 'dja get any love letters from him yet—or did he drop ya like a hot potato?"

"Martina told me that Ari and Danny sent away for X-ray glasses and then looked at each other!" added Tara. "What does Danny look like naked, Ari?" The two girls snorted and laughed.

Ari felt the anger burning in her cheeks. As the hilly sidewalk became steeper, she could hear the sound of her shoes *thwap-thwap*ping louder and faster on the slushy sidewalk.

"Poor Ara-*idne*. She doesn't have her boyfriend to play with anymore!"

"Ari-*odd*-knee! You're such an oddball!" Danielle and Tara's *thwap*ping feet came closer and closer as they too sped up. Just as they were close enough to touch her, Ari whirled around, catching them up short and making Danielle slip and fall into the slush. As Tara tripped over Danielle, her hands and knees also sank into the sloppy gray wetness.

"At least," spat Ari, "I'm nobody's *Winkie*." Thoroughly enjoying the sight of Danielle brushing off her slushy, wet backside and Tara's eyes bugging out in shock, Ari turned and continued walking home.

Her heart was drumming so loudly in her ears, she could barely hear when Tara got up and yelled, "What's that supposed to mean, Odd-knee?"

Ari didn't turn around. She lifted her head into the air and shouted so the kids on the other side of the street could hear: "Winkies are those weird flying monkeys that work for the Wicked Witch of the West. That's what you two are—Winkies! You'll do whatever the Wicked Ole Wallhoffer says!"

Tara caught up and grabbed Ari, and before she had time to think, Ari turned, and her fist swung out and landed with a hard, loud *thwuck* on Tara's stomach. Tara stumbled back and fell into the snow, and for a second they stared silently at each other, trying to absorb what had just happened. But then Ari heard a whoop of laughter from the kids across the street. She felt a flash of lightning through her body and broke into a sprint. The sidewalk was icy in parts, and when she felt she might slip, she threw her arms out like wings, pushing the air away and gliding down the rest of the hill. When she reached the bottom, she took her right turn to head up Highland Avenue and looked over her shoulder. Tara and Danielle were gone, at least for the weekend.

When she pushed open her front door, she still felt as if she were on fire. She bounded up the stairs to her room. Sparks were flying out of her, and she needed to aim them somewhere. Her cheeks and nose were still pink and tingling when she grabbed her yellow legal pad, dove into her reading niche, and started a letter to Danny.

Hi!

Get any good mail these days? I figured you'd like getting mail more than a phone call. I know I do (hint, hint). You won't believe this, but those magic potions work! I put some in Lydia's soda for two weeks, and she started to turn into a walrus! If we lived in the Arctic, she'd have had teenage boy walruses drooling—I'm not kidding. She

145

still won't speak to me, but she is starting to grunt a little. The real bummer is that my parents threw away the rest of the potions and now I'm flat broke for eternity.

I called a psychic named Cassandra (I told you I'd get up the nerve one day) and she predicted a lot of true things, and some not true. She says we're still connected, which was pretty amazing because I never even mentioned our gum-wrapper chain.

Could you believe what a jerk that Wallhopper is? HOLY VOCABULARY, Batman! Who does she think she is—Veronica?!! (Oh, Archikins!) That was a really jerky day when we went bowling, and I'm sorry for having been such a megajerk.

We're doing mythology projects at school. I'm in a group with Hannah and Clarinda. Hannah doesn't just know about trapezoids, she knows The Wizard of Oz, too! Can you believe it? Hannah THE BRAINIAC?! How's gymnastics? Has the King of the Sea Monkeys arrived? Did your other Sea Monkeys have any babies yet? You'd better make me their godmother if they do. Does the trash compactor in your new house work? Does a career in refrigerator repair sound like a thrilling future for Miss Ariadne Spire? For the answers to these and other exciting questions, stay tuned to LOVE OF MAIL*!!!*

Gotta go!

Ari

P.S. My side of the gum-wrapper chain has grown 9 7/16 inches since you moved. How about your side?

Ari licked the envelope, pounded it closed with her fist, and on the outside wrote in clear red marker:

D-liver
D-letter
D-sooner
D-better

Then she ran downstairs and placed it in the mailbox so that the box looked as if it were sticking out its tongue.

Chapter

16

The Greek mythology project began to take shape the next morning when Ari and Clarinda met at Hannah's house.

"My esteemed colleagues," Hannah greeted them with a smile. "Come on in."

"I can only stay till lunch," Clarinda announced. "I've got rehearsals all afternoon for *A Midsummer Night's Dream*. I'm Peaseblossom."

Hannah and Ari melted at the name.

"Who's Peaseblossom?" asked Hannah. Clarinda took her time unwinding the blue-green muffler wrapped around her neck like a giant serpent.

"Oh, one of the woodland sprites," she finally said. "It's a kind of fairy. We sort of flit around the woods whenever Titania, the fairy queen, comes onstage." Clarinda spread her arms, one pointing up and one pointing down, her fingers frozen in a moment of flittering. Ari couldn't figure out how she did it, but right before their eyes Clarinda had become a woodland sprite. She was standing perfectly still, her long scarf hanging around her neck and reaching down to her knees. Yet she looked so different from a minute earlier. It's her fingers, thought Ari. She can make fairy fingers.

"Do you ever get nervous?" asked Hannah, tossing their coats over a large chair in the living room.

"Huh?" said Clarinda, as though the idea had never occurred to her.

"Y'know, scared that you'll make a mistake in front of a huge audience?"

"Not so far," Clarinda said, and blushed. "But I'll tell you something. When we have a test in school, I am *so* pitiful. Nothing but a stomach looking for a place to heave!" Clarinda acted this out, and all three burst out laughing.

Hannah lived on the second and third floors of a two-family house. The furniture was old and a little shabby, and all the rooms they passed were dark. Still, the house was tidy and well cared for. It reminded Ari of her old, beloved slippers. When Hannah led them through the dining room, however, Ari and Clarinda gave a small gasp. Sitting in the dark on a table against the wall were five miniature rooms, complete with intricate moldings, tiny brass doorknobs, and delicate furniture arranged on elaborate rugs scattered across the perfect tiny wooden planks of the miniature oak floor. There were no dolls, just beautiful, empty rooms, like tiny theater sets. Ari had never seen anything like it.

Ari and Clarinda walked gingerly toward the rooms, afraid that normal steps would bring the whole setup crashing to the floor.

"What a great dollhouse!" exclaimed Clarinda.

"Wrong," said Hannah flatly. "These are miniature rooms." Ari and Clarinda looked confused. "A dollhouse is a *house*," explained Hannah, "but these are individual rooms. I inherited them from my great-grandfather, a plumber by day and miniaturist by night." Hannah sounded slightly annoyed and bored, like a tour guide who's recited the same information eleventy-jillion times.

Ari couldn't take her eyes off the rooms. "They're extraordinary," she whispered.

"Thanks. Not that I made them, I mean. It's really my great-grandfather who deserves the credit. But I'll show you something I've been working on." Hannah fooled with something in back of one of the lower rooms. Suddenly the dining room was illuminated by tiny lamps and wall sconces the size of a dime.

"Oh-h-h," mooed Ari and Clarinda, as if they were seeing electricity for the very first time.

"It's taken me a while, but I plan to electrify all the rooms. It isn't easy, though, with the *family* always on my back. They're afraid I'm going to rip up the wallpaper and floorboards and upset the authenticity." Ari and Clarinda were squatting in front of the twinkling room. They looked up at Hannah in disbelief.

"See, these rooms are kind of like the family jewels," she explained, with a few nervous swipes at her hair. It finally stayed behind her ear. "Personally, I think my great-grandfather would be glad I'm doing this." She shrugged, disconnected the wires, and started out of the room. Hannah stopped suddenly and turned around with her hands on her hips, waiting for Ari and Clarinda. Reluctantly the girls stood up and followed her back to the living room.

Two plates of blueberry muffins and many glasses of orange juice later, Ari, Hannah, and Clarinda had some solid plans for their project. They had agreed to write a brief Greek drama that would depict one of the myths they'd read in class. Clarinda would dance the part of Perseus, who sets off to slay the horrible Gorgon. The Gorgon is a creature with snakes sprouting out of her head. Anyone who looks at her is instantly turned into stone. Hannah sug-

151

gested they make masks to represent the different characters, the way people did back in ancient times. Ari would be Athena, the goddess of wisdom, who gives Perseus a mirrored shield for protection.

"And I'll be the Greek chorus," said Hannah. The chorus acted as a kind of narrator for the play.

"Wait a minute," said Clarinda. "Who's going to be the Gorgon?" The girls were silent for a moment, and then Ari suggested they pick someone from the class audience.

"Atwood'll love it," she said. "Who should we choose?"

"Peter Martindale," offered Clarinda. "I don't like his face."

"No, no," said Hannah. "How about . . . Mrs. Atwood?" They all fell on the living room floor, screeching with laughter.

"Wait! Wait!" yelled Ari, barely able to catch her breath. She tried to pull her lips into a serious face. "There's only one person who truly fits this role—Martina Wallhoffer."

"Yes!" shouted Hannah.

"Typecasting," added Clarinda. "Now there's a girl with a poison personality!"

"Poison personality. I've never heard that before, but it fits!" Hannah smiled.

"Well, see, when I first took ballet," Clarinda explained, "my teacher, Miss Beaufont, always used to say it was important to have *poise* and *personality* whenever we danced." Clarinda stuck her chin in the air and made a teacher face. " 'Poise and personality, girls! Poise and personality!' I was only four and I thought she was saying, *'Poison personality'*!" Hannah and Ari giggled. Clarinda blushed. "I could never understand why she wanted us to look like poison, but for a whole year, whenever we had recitals, I would dance with this mean old frown on my face!"

"I can't wait to see Martina wearing a really gross mask with lots of snakes coming out of her head!" said Hannah, waving her fingers in a creepy-crawly dance.

"Me too," Ari agreed, twining her wiggling fingers into Hannah's.

When it was time for Clarinda to leave, Hannah suggested that she and Ari start writing the script that afternoon. They would all meet the next week to make the papier-mâché masks.

"This is going to be really great," Clarinda said as she pulled on her coat and wound her scarf up to her nose like a mummy's wrappings.

"Do some good flittering today," said Ari, and once again Clarinda raised her fairy hands into the air, then departed beautifully.

When the door had closed, Hannah turned and

Ari followed her into the kitchen. Hannah took out a box of frozen pizza. Then she cocked her head like a bird listening for a sound and looked at Ari. "How come you don't call yourself Ariadne? It's such a pretty name."

Ari shrugged. "I always thought people would think it's weird," she replied.

Hannah frowned thoughtfully. "It *is* different, but it's not weird." Hannah slid her fingernail under the box flap and took out the pizza.

Ari silently watched. She had never thought about the difference between being different and being weird. Finally she said, "After lunch can we go back and look at the dollhou—" Hannah sucked in her cheeks and looked at Ari as though she had said a dirty word. "I mean, the rooms," Ari corrected herself. "They're so amazing."

Hannah nodded. "If you have a good box at home, I could show you how to make it into a room," she said. "We could paper it, wire it—everything." Ari's heart raced. The thought of her own miniature room was almost as thrilling as violet contact lenses.

Ari looked at Hannah in wonder. "Everyone thinks your only passion is reciprocal fractions. How come you never mentioned your amazing little rooms?"

Hannah tossed the rectangular sheet of frozen pizza into the toaster oven and brought her hand up in a sweeping arc behind her ear. "I don't know," she replied, smiling shyly. "No one ever asked."

Chapter

17

On Monday morning Ari leapt out of bed, cheer-fully greeted her family, and shoveled break-fast down as if she were in a cereal commercial. Mrs. Atwood would be back today.

On the way to school, Ari let Erica Finn catch up with her and told Erica she could have her old Roll-erblades that didn't fit anymore.

When they got to school, Ari stopped for a drink at the water fountain just before the swinging doors that separated the fourth- and fifth-grade class-rooms. Straightening up to wipe her dripping chin, Ari saw a sight that made her freeze: Mrs. Zwort, standing in the fifth-grade hallway, a lime-green nightmare with poofy hair, snapping her fingers and scowling. The words *mean, stupid, constipated,* and *toad* were the first that echoed in Ari's mind, and her stomach did a forward roll. Oh, God, what else had she written about the Zwort in Friday's journal?

This was far worse than being Martina's X-Friend. This was simply the end for Ari Spire. Unless, unless, unless. Her heart raced with the hope that the pile of journals was still safely on the teacher's desk, untouched and unread. After all, why would the Zwort take them home if Mrs. Atwood was expected back at school? There was still time to hope, still time to sneak into the classroom, remove her journal from the pile, and save her life. Quest for Survival, thought Ari, and she quickly pushed through the swinging doors, waited for the nubby lime-green suit to turn around, and dashed by, unnoticed, into her classroom.

Ari headed straight for the teacher's desk, congratulating herself for her excellent work sneaking past the Zwort. She scanned the desk quickly— there were so many different piles, but where were those little blue journals? She gingerly lifted some of the piles; maybe they were under something. Now she was beginning to panic. The journals were gone! Ari didn't know what to do. Leave school immediately? Face the Zwort and watch her name get permanently carved into the blackboard? She had to think, and the classroom, with people streaming in now, was no place to think.

Ari ran out, pounded through the swinging doors, and headed for the bathroom. She never even saw Martina coming and banged right into her.

"Oh, hi, Ari," chirped Martina. She didn't look mad, and she had a weird smell. "I need to talk to you," she began, not quite looking Ari in the eye. "Umm—remember that really great beauty kit we sent away for?"

"What?" said Ari impatiently. She looked past Martina's shoulder and saw that the Zwort was still in the hall. The bell was going to ring any minute now, and Martina wouldn't move out of the way. Ari felt like a Ping-Pong ball between two enemy paddles.

"A beauty kit?" Ari said. "What about it?"

"Well," said Martina hastily, "you should see it— only there's not as much stuff as they said there would be." Ari wished Martina would get to the point. She had to make a plan. And what in the world was that smell?

"Do you smell something?" asked Ari.

Martina's eyes brightened. "It's the perfume from the beauty kit." She smiled, moving right into Ari's face. "Isn't it great?" Martina had a thick, sharp smell that was oddly familiar. Where had Ari smelled it before? The Zwort! It was the same perfume! Ari took a giant step backward.

"Look, Martina," she said quickly, "I really gotta go."

"Well, it's about the kit," Martina fluttered. "I sort of forgot to cancel our subscription after the first kit came, and I thought, since we're sharing it—remember when I came over to your house and we were looking at comics together?—you should know how much your part costs." Martina thrust a slip of paper at Ari and shook her hair back. "You owe fifteen dollars and twenty-seven cents. That's what it costs to make this month's beauty statement."

The bell rang, and the hall filled with the sounds of doorstops being kicked up and classroom doors squeaking closed. Ari grabbed the bill from Martina. *Fifteen dollars!*

"You've got to be kidding, Martina. I told you I didn't want to send away for it. You can make your own beauty statement." Ari tossed the bill on the floor and turned away. As Martina dove to the floor to rescue the bill, her fingers got stepped on by kids rushing by.

"You better pay your part, Ari!" yelled Martina. "You owe me!" Ari ignored her and kept walking toward the swinging doors. The halls were almost empty. Thanks to Martina, she had no time to do anything but face the Zwort.

159

"Listen, Ari*adenoids*—" Martina's voice had shifted from pleading to nasty.

Ari whipped around. "No. You listen!" she snapped. "You sent away for it—you pay for it! Oz has spoken! Out of my way!" She pushed open the swinging hall doors with both hands and left Martina and her cloud of perfume on the other side of the hall.

Ari entered her classroom, stiff as a zombie. She glanced over at the teacher's desk, but Mrs. Zwort wasn't there. Maybe she was hiding in the cloakroom, taking pleasure in making Ari's agony last as long as possible. Ari went in to hang up her jacket, and as she did, she glanced around for the Zwort. Her fear was making her think ridiculous things, she knew. Maybe if she just pretended nothing was wrong, the Zwort would forget about the journal. *Be a Normal Kid . . . Or Just Look Like One*, thought Ari, and headed for her desk. While her back was turned, she heard the familiar creak of the classroom door. Ari slithered into her seat, and when she looked up, Mrs. Atwood was standing in the doorway, smiling like a teacher goddess.

In one hand she held her favorite Viola Swamp mug, steaming with hot coffee. In her other arm she carried her black attendance book, a folder full of papers, and on top of that, a pile of floppy blue books: the journals!

A small sound came out of Ari that was somewhere between a sigh and a laugh. For the first time she thought to look at the board and noticed that all the names had been erased. Only when she squinted could Ari see the pale record of her days as *Ara-idne*.

"Good morning," said Mrs. Atwood. "It's great to be back." Ari felt warm and happy inside, as though the past two weeks had simply been a bad dream. Everyone started talking at once, entertaining Mrs. Atwood with imitations of the Zwort, until Mrs. Atwood put her finger over her mouth to hush them. "She's substituting right next door," she warned, and Brian Tucker stopped sashaying down the length of the blackboard, where he had written his name followed by an absurdly long tail of check marks.

Seeing Mrs. Atwood again made Ari regret writing all those terrible things. Probably Mrs. Atwood thought Ari was a big, mean, whiny baby. Why hadn't she just ripped out those pages? But maybe Mrs. Atwood hadn't read the journals yet. After all, she wasn't here on the weekend. She couldn't have read them.

As soon as they finished saying the Pledge of Allegience, Ari went up to the teacher's desk, where Mrs. Atwood was handing back piles of corrected tests and papers.

"I'm really glad you're back," said Ari. "I don't think I could've looked at another crossword puzzle." She crossed her eyes as proof. "And those daily word searches—they were the worst. I am totally cured of ever wanting to circle words backward, on the diagonal!"

Mrs. Atwood laughed, and Ari felt relieved. If she had read the journals, she wouldn't have laughed. Still, Ari wanted her journal back in her own hands, and she tried to sound light and breezy when she asked, "Could I see my journal for a minute? I want to write about the dinner we had at my aunt and uncle's house. It was so weird. For dessert, they served this totally melted ice-cream cake, but they never said, 'Oh, sorry, the ice cream melted.' They just acted like it was *supposed* to be melted, and we all had to eat it from our plates like soup!"

Mrs. Atwood smiled and said, "Sure, Ari. I want all the details." She flipped through the books and handed Ari's to her. Ari raced to her seat and opened her journal with her left arm wrapped around it so no one could see. She turned the pages gently, as if defusing a bomb, till she got to the right page. Her eye flew down past her last entry, and she swallowed hard when she saw the familiar slanted handwriting.

Ari,

I'm sorry I was gone so long. I thought Mrs. Zwort had let you know that my mother was sick and needed me while she was in the hospital. I'll try to see that a different substitute takes my classes in the future. I'm also sorry to hear that you've been having a bad couple of weeks. It must be hard not having Danny around. You can still hold on to your friendship, but nothing that grows stays exactly the same, including you. All your life, there are going to be changes, and some of them will make you wish you could just stop time. But there are others, Ariadne, that will surprise and delight even you.

Ari felt as if the wind had been knocked out of her. She watched her teacher rise from her chair, run her fingers through the left side of her hair, and take center stage in front of the board. Mrs. Atwood caught Ari staring, and as her teacher lowered her chin in the tiniest nod, Ari also noticed a small smile aimed in her direction.

Ari sat up straight and took a deep breath, and everything in her classroom—the walls covered with posters and construction-paper projects, the desks filled with wiggling bodies, the big ugly lights that stretched across the ceiling, and the coathanger mobiles that bobbed gently from those lights—everything looked bright and clear.

"Well, now that you've collectively circled every word in the English language backward, sideways, and upside down, let's sharpen our brains and do some real work." Mrs. Atwood turned to write the word *mythology* on the board, and her silver bracelet of a thousand tiny beads made a friendly jingle as her hand moved.

The air in the classroom was back to normal, and when Ari strolled over to the pencil sharpener, she wasn't even bothered by the sight of Martina busily folding her first note of the day, pressing razor-sharp creases into the paper with her thumbnail. Ari passed Tara and Danielle, who widened their eyes and watched her. When Ari returned to her desk, there was a note waiting for her. The piece of loose-leaf paper had been folded over a billion times. Ari quickly unfolded the note.

Dear Ari,

It was fun at Hannah's. I wish I could've stayed longer. I was also wondering if you'd like to come with me to a recital at my dance school next month? There's all these different kinds of dance classes that show off for the parents. Some of them are really good and some of them make you want to laugh like crazy. It's really fun. Check one:

(a) Will come, but can't promise I won't laugh my head off.

(b) Sorry, I wouldn't be caught dead at a dance recital.

Clarinda

Ari smiled to herself, checked (a), and added: *P.S. Maybe you could come to my house this week? I need to know more about Peaseblossom and Titania.* Then she handed the note across the sea of desks to Clarinda on the other side of the room.

Chapter

18

"Mail call!" Lydia sang out, waving a white business envelope in the air. "And for once it's not from some place like Linoleum, New Jersey."

Ari recognized the handwriting right away but didn't want to appear too eager in front of Lydia. She turned back to the mirror.

"I think it's from Danny," said Lydia, squinting to see through the envelope.

"Give it!" yelled Ari, trying to snatch the letter. Lydia raised the envelope high over Ari's head.

"I'm not sure that's the best idea," teased Lydia. "You and Danny might be plotting to send away for a make-your-own thermonuclear device."

"I don't even know what that is," Ari shot back.

"And besides, I apologized for the passion potion in three different languages, and did your chores forever. So give it!"

"So give it!" Lydia mimicked, dropped the letter on the hallway floor, and slithered away.

Ari grabbed it, ran to her room, and shut the door. She scrunched down into her reading niche and studied the handwriting. Then carefully, nervously, she opened the envelope.

Hey there,

Thanks for writing. It was good to get mail. I'm STILL waiting for my Swiss Army Mini Deluxe knife to arrive. Should be any day now.

Guess what? I'm going to be in a movie! (Maybe.) One of the guy's dads on my gymnastic team works in the movie business (REALLY!) and they need kids (boys) who can do gymnastics for some musical number. I get to go to Chicago for the tryouts. I don't get to say anything, but the money is good and who knows, shweethaht, this could be the beginning of a whole new career! (Ouch!!!!)

Keep away from mega-snots like Wallhopper. We're having an interschool meet next Saturday. If you wanna come, bring your own Milk Duds!

Over and out,
Danny

P.S. All but four Sea Monkeys have gone to Sea Monkey heaven. Maybe that's what happens when there's no king.

P.P.S. Gum-wrapper chain so-so.

Ari couldn't believe it. Danny was going to be in a movie! Maybe. Next thing she knew, he'd be living in Hollywood having his nose hairs removed! Gymnastics in the movies? What was this? Just because he could flip in the air like some kind of Sea Monkey, he got to be in the movies? It wasn't fair. Would his address be listed in *Star Daze*? Could he become one of the Faves in the Write to Your Faves! fan club list? Ari felt hot with jealousy. She pulled her soggy hair out of her mouth, put the letter back in the envelope, and went downstairs. She needed to be away from it for a while.

After dinner Ari went back to her room and read the letter again. She sat on her bed this time and turned on the bright reading lamp that was clamped onto the headboard. All Danny's words were still there, but this time Ari felt different. She felt excited for him, and smiled when she pictured Danny saying the word *mega-snots* with one side of his upper lip rising in disgust. And he never said anything about moving away or Hollywood. Most important, he wanted her to come and see him at the meet. The world couldn't keep her away.

Chapter

19

"Why does Lydia have to come?" Ari grumbled as her father started the car. Mr. Spire was dropping Ari and Lydia off at the Winchester High School gym.

"Because Lydia has friends she'd like to see," Mr. Spire said, and Lydia nodded quickly. Ari slumped down in the backseat and sucked on the end of her hair. She knew her father was telling a big fat lie, and that her parents only wanted Lydia along to baby-sit. She grabbed one of the headrests and leaned forward against the front seat.

"I'm not a baby, y'know. I'm almost twelve. I'm on the Brink of Adolescence." She angrily launched herself back into her seat.

Ari's father sighed. "And I'm on the brink of a

midlife crisis. It's hard enough watching my girls grow up so fast. Do you have to keep reminding me?"

The high-school gym sounded like the animal houses at the zoo, with strange growls and screeches jumping out from all sides, then echoing in the distance. It took a while before Ari could pick out Danny from the swinging, vaulting figures below, and when she did, he already looked as if he could be in a movie. Swinging up, over, and under the parallel bars in his white tank top and white leggings, Danny was smaller than most of the other boys, but his movements were smooth and confident.

The teams went through all the required routines, and when Danny finished his set, the gym was full of applause and whistling. Ari finally spotted Danny's mother in the bleachers sitting next to Frank, beaming and turning around to accept compliments from the people behind her.

"C'mon," said Ari, pulling Lydia along the bleachers. "Let's go say hi to Danny's mom and Frank. They'll know where to meet him."

Ari jostled through the crowds around to the other side of the gym. When Ari found Mrs. Ryder, they fell into a tight, rocking hug. Mrs. Ryder's sweater still smelled like Danny's old house. Ari looked up and smiled at Frank. She'd only met him a few times before. He was bald, with a thick brown beard and eyes that crinkled in a friendly way through his glasses. Ari said a shy hello.

"The locker rooms are this way," shouted Danny's mother, as Ari and Lydia followed her down a ramp and out of the gym. They waited in the hallway with other families and friends, and when Danny came sauntering out, Ari felt her heart jump. Danny's mother waved him over, and he sashayed through the bodies, flushed and smiling. His mother gave him a quick hug, and Lydia tousled his hair, saying, "Congrats! Your team deserved to win. And *you* were great, pipsqueak! Watch out, Hollywood!"

"Thanks for coming," he said to Ari.

"You were really good." They were silent for a moment. Ari didn't know what to say next, so she pulled out her program and thrust it in his face. "Can I have your autograph?" she asked like a dreamy-eyed fan.

"Get outta here!" He pushed the paper back in her face.

"Well, why don't we all get out of here," his mother said, steering them by the shoulders. "Who's up for ice cream?"

"Me!" shouted Danny and Ari. Then, bumping Ari's arm with his elbow, he said, "I could really go for a dish of Chicken Fat Ripple! How 'bout you?"

"It's always a good time for Kitty Litter Crunch in a cone!"

"You two are incredibly warped," said Lydia, and shared a look with Danny's mother.

When they arrived at the ice-cream parlor, Danny's mother suggested that she and Frank and Lydia take one booth and Danny and Ari take another. Ari could've kissed her.

"So tell me about your new movie career," Ari said, digging her long-handled spoon into Chocolate Mocha Madness, Fudge Brownie Frenzy, and Triple Threat Oreo Crunch ice cream, with hot fudge, marshmallow, and whipped cream.

"It's not so much," Danny mumbled around the spoon in his mouth. "It's some musical that takes place in New York City a long time ago." He dug the long spoon into the sundae glass and scraped the side where all the caramel had settled.

"There's a big number they do in the streets and they need kids to flip over vegetable carts and do cartwheels on rooftops—that sort of thing. To tell you the truth, the reason they want me"—the spoon dove back in on the other side of the glass to rescue the hot fudge that was turning cold and hard—"is because I'm—short."

"Huh?"

"Scott's dad said I look a lot younger than I really

am. And they want it to look like these young kids are doing all this slick jumping around."

"Oh." Ari had wolfed down her sundae, and now she was eyeing Danny's. Danny looked anxious to stop talking and get back to his ice cream before it melted into liquidy goop.

"When are you going to Chicago?"

"End of next week."

"Next *week*? Wow!"

"Yeah. We're gonna stay with my cousins. It's gonna be great." Ari gave him a moment of silence, allowing him to scrape out the last of the ice cream.

"Hey," said Ari, "did you ever see a movie called *Singin' in the Rain*? It's my new favorite. What a hoot—the musical numbers are the *best*."

Danny looked up. "What happened to *The Wizard of Oz*?"

"Well, I still think it's one of the greats in movie history," Ari said thoughtfully, "but it's time to move on, y'know?" Danny licked the back of his spoon and nodded.

"Uh-huh. I'm into Hitchcock films now. Maybe you could come over and we could watch *Vertigo*. And you could see the new house. There's this great climbing tree in our neighbor's yard. It'd be great for Quest for Survival."

Ari smiled. "Definitely."

Lydia waved to a group of friends at another booth, and kept torturing Ari by constantly pointing at her sitting with Danny. Danny's mother finally released Lydia to her friends, and Ari was invited back to Winchester.

When they got to Danny's house, he demonstrated the trash compactor for her. Then he led her into the next yard to show her the massive beech tree.

"Mark, set, go!" he shouted, and sped off toward the tree. They were high in the branches when it occurred to Ari that they had forgotten the bread and cheese.

"Want me to go get it?" said Danny, already sliding down to a lower branch.

"No, that's okay. I'm not really hungry, anyway."

"Mmm. Me neither."

Then Ari said, "Remember when we were Hansel and Gretel and you actually ate some weird berries I pulled off the front hedges?" Danny poked at the bark of the tree with a short stick and smiled.

"Well, you dared me to."

"Did not."

"You said it would be our only food for days!"

"That's not daring you!"

"Yeah, just threatening me! God, was I sick. A regular barfathon that night!"

Ari laughed. "I think that's when we started using bread and cheese!" They sat for a while without saying anything. Ari shredded a leaf down to its skeleton while Danny examined an insect on the tip of his stick. They both knew they weren't going to play Quest for Survival anymore. Ari looked at Danny and suddenly an old playground taunt popped into her head: "Ari and Danny sittin' in a tree, K-I-S-S-I—"

"Show me your room," Ari blurted, trying to blot out the song in her brain.

"Okay." Danny scampered down the branches and jumped to the ground. Ari followed him.

Danny still had his raggy blue bedspread, but all around the room were large, shiny posters from past Olympics picturing famous male gymnasts. The gum-wrapper chain was nowhere to be seen, and something about all those posters with their bright colors and determined-looking athletes told Ari: Don't ask about it. Instead she said, "Hey, why don't we pull out the ole Ouija board and see if you're going to get that part in the movie?" They sat on the floor and balanced the board between them, as always. The indicator slid to *Y*. Ari narrowed her eyes at Danny.

"You're sure you're not moving it?" she asked.

"I swear—on John Wayne's grave—I'm not." The

indicator moved to *E,* and Ari watched Danny's hands even more closely. Then it slid over to *R.* It made a move backward to *P* and stopped.

"YERP? What's that supposed to mean?"

Danny picked up the indicator and wiped the needle with a damp finger. "Maybe this thing's dirty," he said. "Maybe it really meant to stop at *S.*"

"Maybe. Unless it just isn't sure what will happen. Even a Ouija board can have an off day."

Danny smiled and quickly grabbed the board and threw it into the closet.

"I guess you'll just have to write and let me know. Mail for Ms. Ari Spire!"

Danny snorted a laugh and then got something from the top drawer of his dresser. He turned around with his arm extended toward her, his hand balled in a tight fist. His hand opened.

"The Swiss Army Mini Deluxe!" cried Ari. "At last, your Swiss oatmeal days are over!"

Danny nodded, smiling. "Lookit," he said, and one by one showed her all the gadgets. It had a compass, a corkscrew, scissors, magnifying glass, tiny flashlight, nail file, can opener—and there was the fishing line, with a small hook at the end.

Ari was impressed. "It's got everything you need for survival," she said excitedly. "The only thing missing is a *little teeny* piece of bread and cheese!"

"Yep," said Danny, tossing it into the air and

catching it with one hand. "It's got it all." He let Ari pull out all the gadgets. When she handed it back to him, he seemed relieved.

Danny tossed his knife from hand to hand. "My dad says we might take a fishing trip this summer."

"Hey, you can try out the fishing line!" Ari said.

"Maybe," replied Danny. He turned the Swiss Army Mini Deluxe over and over in his hands. "My dad really likes fishing."

Ari watched Danny thinking. "Hey," she said, "maybe you'll catch us the King of the Sea Monkeys!"

"Speaking of which," he said slowly, "do you think you could, um, look after those guys while I'm away?" He gestured with his head toward the fishbowl.

"Can't you just throw in a mess of Sea Monkey food and let 'em go at it for a few days?"

"No way. That'll do 'em in for sure."

Ari walked over to the bowl for a moment and stared at the water, trying to find something lovable in the tiny life-forms. Mega–rip-off is right, she thought. But to Danny she said, "Okay," and he looked really happy.

"It's important that I don't ditch 'em," said Danny. "See, I have to prove to my mom that I'm serious about taking care of a pet. I figure I'm kind of working my way up the food chain, right? So the next time I ask her for a pet, maybe I'll get something you can see without a microscope!"

"Yeah," laughed Ari. "By the time you're thirteen you'll be having great fun walking your pet grass-hopper."

Ari knew she probably wouldn't see Danny before his Chicago trip, so when her mother came to pick her up, she walked carefully down the stairs holding a cottage cheese container full of Sea Monkeys.

Ari walked out the front door, then turned around. "Hey, pardner," she said, "good luck out in there in the tall and uncut."

Danny smiled. "Same to you, shweethaht," he said, closing the door before Ari could sock him.

When she got home, Ari set the Sea Monkeys on her desk and gave them names of old movie stars. She knew she'd never be able to tell them apart, but they were kind of like pets, after all, and it seemed the right thing to do.

Then she went to her closet and took out the box that held the gum-wrapper chain. As she placed the box on the floor, she thought of Hannah, remembering her offer to help Ari make a miniature room of her own. Ari opened the box, dumped out the gum-wrapper chain, and examined the empty box for possibilities. It was perfect. Holding the box in her lap, Ari felt the thrill of the days ahead, of spending hours with Hannah transforming the plain box. It was a project they could share, something to look forward to, just as she and Danny had imagined the day they would dial up *The Guinness Book of World Records* and say triumphantly, "We have a world record to report." Ari's hands stroked the top of the box, and she opened it again, her mind whirling with excitement now as she imagined the tiny, illuminated world that was waiting to be created.

Putting the box aside, Ari picked up the paper chain and draped a part of it over her hands. As she studied the intricate braid of colors and letters, it seemed almost magical how a simple fold had transformed these ordinary paper scraps into a beautiful design. Nothing she and Danny had ever sent away for was as wonderful as the thick, smooth zigzags in her lap. Her stomach tightened a little at the thought of not adding any more links, of changing the box into something special she would share with Hannah, not Danny. It was strange, but after visiting his new house and hearing about all the new things happening in his life, the days of rescuing Danny from Minotaurs and Cyclopses, of feeling lost in the maze herself, suddenly felt very far away.

Running her hands lightly over the colorful chain, Ari looked up at her ceiling, covered with glow-in-the-dark stars, and knew exactly what she wanted to do.

Holding an open box of thumbtacks in one hand and the gum-wrapper chain in the other, she stood on her bed, then climbed onto the radiator, over to the top of her desk, and onto her dresser, pinning the paper chain in a circle around her room. When she finally reached the end, she tacked the last colorful zigzag onto the ceiling molding so that it neatly joined the rest of the chain.

Ari closed the box of thumbtacks, jumped down from the radiator, and wiped the side of her hand across her damp forehead. Then she flopped down dizzily onto her bed, her heart pounding as she tucked her hands behind her head and gazed up at Ariadne's crown overhead.

20

It was Saturday and a perfect spring day. Lydia was on the front steps reading when Ari flounced out the door, singing, "I just know there's mail for me today!" and flipped open the top of the mailbox. "Wait a minute." Ari dug the Magic Eight Ball key chain out of her pocket, closed her eyes, and asked, "Will there be mail for me today?" She turned over the ball. " 'It Is Decidedly So.' All right!" Lydia ignored her as Ari's hand dove into the mailbox and pulled out a postcard. It was from Chicago. "See, Lyd, it worked!"

Ari turned the card over and read the one word written in giant red Magic Marker letters: "YERP!!!!" She said it aloud to herself and smiled. Then at the bottom of the postcard, in tiny pencil letters, she read: "P.S. You would really like Chicago."

"Danny's going to be in the movies! In a musical!" Ari yelled to Lydia. Lydia turned around with her mouth open.

"What else does he say?" asked Lydia, amazed. "When are they gonna start? Does he have a speaking part?"

"I don't know. No details yet. All it says is that he got the part and that he wishes I were in Chicago with him." Lydia widened her eyes, and Ari smiled smugly. She had to share the news with someone immediately, someone good. Maybe Hannah was home. Or Clarinda. She needed to celebrate. Maybe go for ice cream and pick up the latest *Weekly Comet*. Lydia kept asking questions, but her voice was drowned out by the sounds of Ari slamming the screen door as she ran inside for money, yelling: *"Yerp! Yerp! Yerp!"*

A moment later Ari was bounding out of the house, half a Pop-Tart in her hand. "Well, I'm off!" she announced to Lydia, as if she were on her way to Cairo. "Tell Mom I took the bus to Hannah's."

"Hmm-kay," hummed Lydia, her nose back in her book. Jumping off the porch, Ari noticed a bright yellow gum wrapper flapping in the dirt by the hedges. She registered the specimen—a Juicy

Fruit—and saw a bird hopping around the yellow paper as if considering it for a decorative touch to its nest. Ari headed for the gum wrapper, ready, as usual, to scoop it right up. But then she remembered, and she stopped. There wasn't any gum-wrapper chain reaching toward Danny anymore. Instead, she had changed it so that it could be a crown among the stars. Mrs. Atwood was right. Some changes could really surprise you.

A gentle wind blew the gum wrapper to Ari's feet. Then Ari broke off a piece of Pop-Tart, and as she crumbled it on the ground, she addressed the bird:

"WELCOME TO *LIFESTYLES OF FRIENDS OF THE NEARLY RICH AND FAMOUS*! TODAY WE CATCH UP WITH ARIADNE SPIRE AS SHE TAKES TIME OUT FROM HER FASCINATING CAREER IN REFRIGERATOR REPAIR TO SHARE A PORTION OF HER TOASTER PASTRY WITH A HUMBLE WOODLAND CREATURE. NATURALLY, THIS PHENOMENAL LIFESTYLE IS ONE YOU AND I CAN ONLY DREAM ABOUT. BUT FOR ARIADNE, IT'S A FANTASTIC FAIRY TALE COME TRUE!"

Lydia kept her eyes on her book, but Ari saw her sister shaking her head and grinning. The bird picked up the largest crumb and flew behind the hedges, where it was greeted by a chirping ruckus. Then Ari picked up the gum wrapper and waved it in front of Lydia's face.

"Here, Lydia. Trash." Ari dropped the wrapper into her sister's lap. "You could recycle this. Who

knows—maybe it'll come back as a bumper sticker."
Ari parted her hands dramatically: "Save Waldo and
Simone!"

"But it's a *gum wrapper*," said Lydia, holding it out
to Ari. "Don't you want it?"

"No thanks," Ari replied. She wiggled her purple
glasses on straight. "I don't need it." Then, starting
off with a little hop, Ariadne bounded down the
street toward the bus stop on the corner.